MW01134797

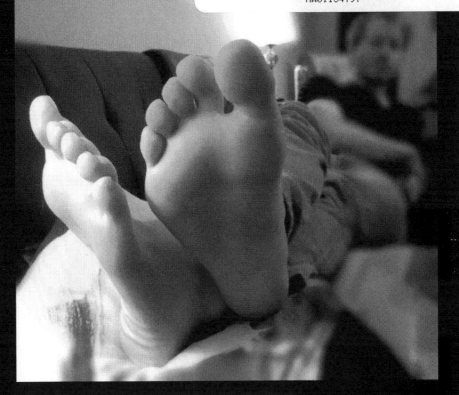

ROOMMATE.
MASTER.
FOOTGOD.
KING.

a James T. Medak novel

ROOMMATE. MASTER. FOOTGOD. KING.

By James T. Medak

NOTE: Under no circumstances should you read this book unless you yourself are barefoot.

TABLE OF CONTENTS

INTRODUCTION

At the end of the day, it's all about power.

My fiancé, ever curious, has been reading a book about human development and noted that we are middle-of-the-foodchain species, one that, for generations, was worried about being eaten by bigger, meaner animals. While we've grown smart and developed tools and created civilizations, that nervousness has still stuck with us, and we overcompensate with capitalism and controlling the environment and ... whatever else we need to do to convince ourselves that we're top-dog.

Yet we're not. We have dominion over some things but honestly crave commands. Orders. Directives. It's not our fault: it's just built into our nature, even if we've spent centuries convincing ourselves otherwise. This is partially because as we go about and manage our day-to-day lives, it's nice to have that sense of release, to not think about things -- to have someone do the thinking for you.

It's for this reason that I've seen doms on Tumblr and Instagram have those occasional bouts of submissive feelings, of wanting to be reminded how bad they are for being so horny. It's a thrilling reversal, each and every time. It's for this reason you also see powerful CEOs and multi-hyphenates often succumb to the call of mistresses and kink bondage sessions: they need a release. After carrying so much of the world on their shoulders and dictating the lives of many, it's sometimes nice to take a back seat and just be told what to do for once.

This idea of power came circling back time and time again in my mind, and it seemed to make for a fitting start for a new story. "Roommate. Master. Footgod. King." was inspired by the plot summary for a French horror film called *Martyrs*, based around a cult that tortured people to experience such blinding pain that they'd eventually see the face of god. While you all know I am 100% not about pain in any way shape or form, something about the idea intrigued me, especially when you thought about placing pain with pleasure. Fountains of pleasure. Overwhelming pleasure with no release. Coupled with the kind of casual verbal mind control exhibited by Kilgrave/The Purple Man from Season 1 of the Netflix Marvel show *Jessica Jones*, something about a too-powerful antagonist against a sweet and innocent straight bro just seemed too good to go unexplored.

Hence, there is chastity, fucking, rimming, humiliation, bondage, and so much more wrapped into a story that is primarily and dominantly about the power of male bare feet and the subjection of one to that power. It's a different tale than ones I've told before, but one that feels very authentic and very, very fun (if even a bit terrifying).

So please, take your shoes and socks off and enjoy. Think about what could've happened with your own roommates, past or present. Don't forget: horny inspiration is every damn where. Use it.

Yours,

James T. Medak
(May 2018)

Dedicated to Bearfoothunter

CHAPTER I: THREE SHARP KNOCKS

Three. Sharp. Knocks.

"Fuck," thought Jon.

The brown-haired 20-something adonis almost wasn't ready for this, having lightly dozed off waiting for another showing. It was a hair past 6pm. He needed a roommate, sure, and he responded to the latest in a seemingly never-ending supply of responses to his Craiglist ad indicating that yeah, today would be good for a showing, but this guy was early. Like, an hour too early. Jon was running around frantically to put his casually-preppy clothes on, eventually settling for a nice white-and-gray striped short sleeve top that nicely accentuated his ever-narrowing waist. Toss on some tight blue jeans and some fitness ankle socks and -- it'll have to do.

He skidded in those socks across the hardwood floor of his massive, 1200-foot second-floor walk-up and buzzed the guy in. It was such a hectic day that, honestly Jon had already forgotten who this new prospect was. Hopefully he was cool. Hopefully he's just not a nebby little weirdo.

He opened the door and heard footsteps going up the carpeted stairs of this meager four-story house, lovingly turned into some rent-controlled profit utopia for landlords. The figure whose head was popping up was ... unusually dapper. By Jon's guess, it was a guy who was in his mid-20s but was exceedingly tall, like almost six-and-a-half feet. He was wearing a dark blue shirt with an even darker-offset purple button vest and a sky-blue tie, almost as if he was showing up expecting it to be a job interview. Short brownish/blondish hair. Thin business glasses. As he reached the landing, the man's stature positively towered over Jon, who stood there somewhat surprised, even with his salon-ready short hair and morning scruff on his face.

"Hey man, I'm Jon. Who are you?" he asked, brightly.

"You'll find out soon enough," said the man, immediately walking into the apartment without even giving so much as a glance to Jon.

The tall man surveyed the land: three bedroom, one bathroom, back porch with stairs that connected to the other neighbors. Not bad. Typical Midwest setup here, but appealing. As he looked around, Jon, a bit shocked by how rude this guy was, and tried to force conversation.

"So, I'm Jon. Your name is ...?"

"Mike," the man said bluntly, still not making eye contact with Jon. "Any problem with neighbors? Noise?"

"Umm, no," Jon said as Mike stood in the living room with the windows facing the street, examining the couches, almost as if he was looking for something. "I sometimes hear the occasional creak of a footstep on the hardwood overhead but I never hear arguments or TV or speakers or nothing."

"Good," Mike said, sitting himself down on the couch with the coffee table in front of it. "I'll take it."

Jon was a bit stunned by Mike's abruptness and presumption. "OK," Jon cautiously started, "I mean, that's great and all, but this is my apartment. My roommate suddenly getting some fucking movie gig has left me in a hell of a bind, so while yes, the sooner the better, I want to make sure that we gel first, you and I. Also, as the ad read, rent is pretty darn--"

"I said I'll take it," Mike said as he leaned over to ... untie his shoes?

Jon arched his eyebrows. What the hell was this guy thinking? "Um, it's a lot of money. I mean, if you got it, great, but they're also threatening maybe raising the rent soon so--"

"It won't be an issue," Mike said, his shoes now loose and open. He put his socked feet up on the coffee table. They were dark business sheer socks, the shadows and accents of his toes seen at just the right angle. Jon couldn't help but notice how overwhelmingly huge these things were: size 14 maybe?

"OK," Jon said, cautiously. "I mean ... listen, you're straightforward, I'll give you that."

With those cloth-covered soles now on the table, all Mike did was just stare at Jon through those thin wire glasses. He simply asked "So, Jon, what is it you don't like about me? You do seem hesitant about letting me stay here, it seems."

At that exact moment, Jon felt something inside him which he couldn't describe. Like the feeling that a finger suddenly pressed on his brain's truth center, against his will, forcing out awkward beliefs that he wouldn't dare say in public.

"I think you're cocky," he sputtered, seemingly amazed at how honest the statement was. "You seem like an asshole and you're behaving really weird and I don't want you here anymore." It was upsetting to Jon to hear how childlike his mutterances were. Mike seemed utterly unphased by the outburst.

"OK. Are you straight? Gay?" Mike inquired.

"Very straight, sir," Jon said, amazed that the "sir" slipped in there. What the actual fuck was happening to his brain right now?!

"Very good," mulled Mike. "I can work with that." Mike glanced around the apartment. "I'm going to take it. I'm going to be your new roommate, Jon. You're going to accept me as your roommate and accept me gladly. How does that sound?"

Jon couldn't believe the gall of this motherfucker, but as soon as Mike stopped speaking, he felt a smile creep onto his face, one that he genuinely did not want on there, and one that would've appeared as genuine to any casual onlooker.

"Oh Mike," Jon blurted out, "Yes! Yes! We're gonna be roommates! I'm so excited!"

Jon's brain was screaming at this, as his words and actions were 100% the opposite of what he was actually feeling. It's like in the span of just a minute he had become some sort of puppet, some sort of voodoo doll hung up on a shelf. Jon was scared and angry at once, hating every second of it and wanted it to stop and why isn't it stopping oh gods it's not stopping?! He was doing everything he could to not have a panic attack as to why his body would do such unbelievably stupid things.

Mike smiled. "I'm glad you're excited, Jon," he said. "This is going to be a great base of operations. I'll leave my current address here. Tomorrow morning call a moving company and pay them in advance to get my things here as soon as possible. I'll leave a key under the outside doormat of my old place. You'll soon be telling the movers just how I like things done."

Jon was still in shock over whatever was happening but knew that ... he ... was going ... to pay for moving Mike in. That was ... going to be hundreds of dollars. Dollars he needs to pay the rent. Why was he going to do this? Why was he just ... agreeing with everything that Mike was saying? It felt like a bad dream. Like some sort of weird nightmare.

"OK," Jon said, confirming apparently everything Mike wanted.

Mike started to reach for his shoes to put back on, but stopped. He instead looked at Jon and smirked. Young, supple body, scruffy hair, might even be a smart boy ... but might not be.

"Jon," Mike started. "Have you ... ever had it up the ass?"

"No," Jon said, amazed by how abrupt his answering of Mike's insane question was, still standing and facing Mike like a goddamn idiot. Mike's eyes drifted down to Jon's shirt, squinting, inquiring.

"Have you ever sucked a dick before?" Mike again probed.

"No," responded Jon, honestly.

"That'll change," said Mike, soon eyeing Jon's slender frame, licking his lips just a bit. "Now tell me about your nipples."

"What ... what about them?" Jon stuttered, going full-blown nervous over the question.

"Are they connected to your dick at all?" Mike inquired. "Like, if you play with them at all, do they get you hard?"

Jon used all the willpower he could not to answer but his mouth didn't care: "Extremely. It's like they're hard-wired to my dick. Anytime a girl starts messing around with them, I get hard in a heartbeat."

Mike smirked. "Good. Now get out your phone." Jon did so. "Get really close to my socked feet here on the table. Get some shots where you can see my toes clearly through these sheers." Again, Jon did so, kneeling on the hardwood while figuring out the best possible shot wherein he would ... get this guys' toes clearly defined? His brain was doing backflips as his body went through the motions, his goofy fucking grin still being on his face, "wanting" Mike to be here. He snapped more than a few photos.

"You enjoy looking at my toes," Mike stated.

"Yes, I really do!" Jon agreed, his grin betraying every fucking fiber of his being.

"Great," started Mike, reaching to put his shoes on for real this time. "Do you have a job tomorrow?"

Jon thought out loud: "Tomorrow is Tuesday so ... no, I have tomorrow off."

"Even better," said Mike, lacing his shoes up and readying himself to leave. "You're going to spend the rest of the night edging yourself and getting hard while looking at that photo of my toes. You're going to start having one hell of a foot fetish. Look at every detail of those photos. The shape of the toes. The textures. The toeprints. Make one of those photos the background on your computer screen. Don't cum, but just stare at my toes and think about how sexy they look and get harder and harder until you're begging yourself for mercy. Actually, let's not be cruel. Do this until 3AM. Then set an alarm for 7AM, and once you wake up, call the moving company."

"Yes, sir," is all Jon could say in return, helpless to the words being spoken before him.

"Alright," said Mike, standing up to leave. "I'll be in touch. Can't wait to be roommates with you." He walked towards the door. "Now," Mike said, hand on the doorknob, "what is it you're supposed to do there, Jon?"

"Upload these photos of your toes onto my computer, make one of them my background, set an alarm for 3AM, and edge myself silly to the shape of your toes until I'm begging myself to cum," said Jon.

"That's right," stated Mike, "except ... one last thing. You will enjoy doing it. You enjoy being my slaveboy. You enjoy getting hard to male feet. You're grateful I've given you this task, OK?"

"Yes, sir," said Jon, still grinning like a fucking idiot.

"Have fun," said Mike as he walked out and closed the door behind him.

Without a second's hesitation, Jon immediately went into his bedroom and plugged his phone into his computer. He slowly extracted each and every photo of Mike's sheer toes that he took and placed them, lovingly, in their own special folder. He eyed them closely, looking for the one that was the most appealing, the most appetizing. Jon's straightboy brain was hyperventilating: *What the fuck are you doing, man?!* But by this point, even his brain couldn't deny the truth: for whatever fucking magic reason, he was completely under the control of the mysterious Mike, and Mike apparently had a thing for feet.

Yet there Jon was, making one of the photos his background image, setting an alarm on his phone, and then setting up the folder that the socks pics were in as a screensaver. Now, all his computer screen would do would switch randomly between the dozen or so photos that he took of Mike's feet every 30 seconds. Jon sat there, transfixed. His brain was beyond traumatized, but his face was happy. Goofily happy. He was staring deeply at Mike's sheer toes, admiring the beauty in the shapes: the long, thick, stem-like nature of the toe base, cropping up from the nicely-angled ball of Mike's size 14 foot. He loved, however, the orb-like nature of Mike's toes, so round and so ... supple. The fact that they were peaking through sheers, and the way the fabric stretched and bent between each toe-tip, was driving Jon crazy. His jeans and boxers were down around his knees, and here he was, stroking his sizable pink cock slowly. Sometimes jerking it, but often just going back to stroking it. Against all odds, here he was, getting physically hard to some dude's fucking toes in sheer socks. He felt like some fucking toy monkey, jackin' himself while looking at something he never gave two seconds thought about before ever in his life.

An hour passed.

His eyes were starting to get a little bleary. It was the same dozen images cycling through, but Jon simply couldn't fucking stop touching his rod, finding new things to like each time one of those toe shots came up in rotation. At this point, he had practically memorized Mike's toes by heart, and his cut cockhead was starting to turn a juicy pinkish red. There was a little dab of precum right at the tip. Jon would sometimes have to switch hands to stop himself from cramping, but the motions were constant: he kept jacking it to Mike's toes, his body lying to his brain by telling it that it actually enjoyed what it was doing.

Four. Sharp. Knocks.

Fuck, though Jon, stroking it in his bedroom to Mike's sheer toes. *Who the fuck is that?* he thought. At first, his heart started quickening, as it was obvious that it had to be Mike, no doubt ready to dole out further commands and torment. Fuck, he didn't have a command to answer the door -- he *had* to keep jacking until 3AM.

The knocks kept happening. Jon was getting nervous, but his eyes were at the screen, his dick was still hard, and that's all that mattered right now. In the back of his mind, he wondered if his old roommate had somehow come back to get his stuff, but he wouldn't be able to face him when he was here 'cos he's under Mike's control and--

"I'm here for the viewing?" shouted a meek voice through the front door.

Goddammit, it was another showing. Jon was troubled 'cos he didn't want anyone to see him under this state in any way shape or form whatsoever but he also wanted help. He wanted the spell of Mike broken so he could go back to a normal life and maybe this was all a fucking weird-ass nightmare but as he stroked his cock it just FELT so real and ...

"C'mon! Is anyone home?" the voice shouted.

Fuck was all that Jon's brain could think of. He tried with all of his might to do *anything* besides jerk his cock while staring at more photos of Mike's sheer toeshapes but his body was stubborn, not allowing his brain even an inch.

"What a fucking ripoff..." the voice mumbled. Jon was upset he couldn't do anything else for the prospect or have the prospect do fucking anything to help him out, but it was only now that Jon realized just how utterly powerful Mike's control over him was. How did he do it? Was he a hypnotist? A real-fucking-life magician? These were all the thoughts Jon could muster when not thinking about the stretchiness of that sheer sock fabric or the undersides and prints of Mike's toes or how much he enjoyed jacking his straightboy six-incher to the very shapes and curves and textures of Mike's toes. In fact, the screensaver restarted, so it was time to keep jacking. Off to the side, he saw his phone light up with Facebook notifications but he couldn't pick up the phone to see what they were: all he was to do was to keep stroking and teasing his dick until 3AM.

Hours passed.

It was now 2:58AM. Jon's eyes were watering a bit, having stared at the screen so much that it feels like Mike's toes were now imprinted on his eyeballs. At this point, his dick was so hard that all he could muster were a few quick tugs to get it excited again before he had to stop 'lest he came. Precum had become so abundant that it had streaked past the rim of his cockhead and down the entirety of his shaft to nestle in his lightly browned patch of crotch-hair. It was almost too much. The worst part was the lightning sensation alive in his rod, filling up his entire body not with desire, but pure, animalistic lust. He wanted to fucking rape his own hand right now in order to shoot out the biggest load of his life, hot sticky seed getting all over his body in an embarrassing fashion that would've felt so good in the moment. But he knew he couldn't. He wasn't told he could, so all he could do was keep edging.

Panicked and weakened, Jon's eyes darted over to his phone. He could see the time switch over from 2:59AM to 3:00AM. His eyes shut. He laid back in his chair. He passed out from exhaustion, his right hand still on his dick, covered in a glaze of precum. He had never been so desirous for sleep, but never in his life ever felt so utterly defeated.

CHAPTER II: OPEN ME

Jon's 7AM alarm was annoying as fuck. Sharp beeps. Sharp, stabbing beeps. Jon's eyes made rolling, rousing movements under his lids, but when he finally opened them, they immediately started watering up, exhausted from staring at his computer screen for so long. He saw that he was still at the computer and that screensaver was still running, those socked toes still flashing by with their shapes, contours, and odd sense of power.

Jon hated seeing that screen, hated noticing that his hands were caked with precum. *What the actual fuck happened yesterday?* he thought. The screensaver, even now, felt like some sort of cruel joke, the remnants of a bad trip or something, but no, there were those images of Mike's feet. Staring right back at him. It was all so surreal.

Yet ... Jon felt free. He saw the images on the screen, and even with the occasional tingle and spark in his groin, he didn't feel compulsory subservient to them. His brain wasn't working against his spirit with zero resistance in the way it felt last night. He was ... normal.

"What the fuck?" he said out loud to no one, still trying to comprehend all that was going on.

Despite being exhausted, he no longer liked being coated in pre, so got in the shower and washed up his athletic, supple body. As the shower head massaged his scalp, Jon's mind went all over the place, at times touching on the bizarre situation from last night and if this is something anyone would believe if he told them to where he was in his life right now. Yeah, he had a simple retail job in a giant city, but he was out of college, had a degree, had a love of music, technology, and cinema. Yet ... that was it. He wanted to get a band going, or maybe help lens someone's film or something, but he felt there was this ... inertia in his life. Yeah, a girlfriend would be great, but with his other buddy actually going to California and pursuing his real film dreams, Jon just felt ... idle? Unproductive? It was hard to define, but it did get to him.

Jon got out of the shower, started drying himself off, and then was struck by more flashes of last night. Wasn't he supposed to do something this morning? Oh yeah, apparently call and pay for Mike's moving expenses. He didn't even know where the fuck Mike lived. Wait, did Mike really just come in here last night and just say he was gonna be the new roommate? *Fuck that*, thought Jon. What the actual fuck did go down last night? The more he thought about it, the angrier he got. *I need a coffee*. Sure, he was still tired as fuck from edging himself like a dumb monkey last night, but he's not gonna let the day defeat him.

Jon quickly threw on some shorts, some tight white ankle socks, some band t-shirt he rarely wears out in public, and some ice-cream white sneakers. He's not gonna let anything ruin his day.

He opened up his apartment door and saw ... a package on the ground. "OPEN ME" it said in handsomely bold black Sharpie letters. It was a sizable package: a big fuckin' envelope with dimensions larger than a clipboard. There were some lumps to it: there was something inside of it. No name or address. His interested piqued, he brought it inside.

Sitting down on his couch, the same one where Mike laid his sheer feet out and started ordering him around like some sort of Metrosexual Mussolini, Jon placed his package down on his wood coffee table. Jon couldn't put his finger on it, but there was something about the package that put him on edge. He would've thought it was delivered to the wrong address had it not been wedged very closely to his specific door. Opening it up, a weird kind of smell came out of the package. Nothing foul, but something ... salty? A bit raw? What the fuck was it?

He shook the contents of the bag out, and there was a black Sharpie, an index card, a mini-cassette player with a note saying "PLAY ME" affixed to it, what appeared to be a brand new smartphone, and ... a pair of ankle socks? White, worn ankle socks? "Fuckin' gross," said Jon aloud, tossing them to the other side of the table. This all seemed profoundly strange, and maybe he shouldn't have, but the curiosity around hitting the tape that said "PLAY ME" was too great. Hit 'play' he did.

"Hello, Jon." Fuck, it was Mike's voice. "You're probably wondering why you're feeling so good and free this morning, and why last night happened. Well, guess what? I haven't forgotten about you. First off, you will let this tape play until the end. You will not pause it or stop it."

Jon was about to laugh at the arrogance of such a suggestion, but ... *holy fuck it kicked in again.* His brain. His body. They betrayed him. Any impulse he had to try and hit pause or stop on that fuckin' little tape device was eradicated. It was gone. This was the exact same frustration he felt last night, and he couldn't believe he fell into this trap. How the living fuck was Mike able to control him?

"There is an index card there with my current address on it. Call a moving company and follow your orders from yesterday, ensuring they get things over to me in as timely a manner as possible. Today if doable. You're paying for it with your credit card, so price shouldn't even be an issue. You're happy to do this for me."

Jon actually grinned upon hearing that. His lying body told him that this was, in fact, something he was happy to do.

"Once you're done with that -- and have eaten and done other, ahem, regular functions -- you will proceed to strip naked, sniff these sweaty, two-day-old socks of mine, and edge yourself again. You will not cum, just like last night. You will edge yourself and get really turned on by my masculine foot smell. It excites you. You couldn't be more excited for the next stroke that follows. Once you feel like you're on the edge of cumming, you will stop, take out the sharpie, and write I AM A FOOTSLAVE over your face, forehead, and multiple times across your chest. You will then pick up this new phone. This phone is a gift from me to you. You will thank me in person for this gift. There is one number saved on it -- it is mine. You will video chat me at that point, your body covered in humiliating ink, and you will beg me for the chance to cum while sniffing my socks. I will want to see every inch of your body beg for this."

Jon glanced over at the socks, now with a hint of fascination in his face, and then back to the tape machine.

"Repeat what you are to do out loud."

"Um," started Jon, "First I'm going to hire movers using my own money to get all of your stuff here in as quick a manner as possible. Then, I'm going to do basic everyday functions for a bit ... then I will strip and edge myself to your smelly socks 'cos they fuckin' turn me on. Once I'm close to cumming, I'll write 'I am a footslave' across my forehead, face, and across my chest. I will then take the phone you have generously gifted me and I will call you and beg for the chance to cum while sniffing your socks."

A few more seconds of blank tape played. Mike recorded a pause in here but it was just a fucking tape: Mike had no idea how long Jon's interpretive recitation of his commands would go.

"Good boy," the tape said. "Now hop to it. I will be in later tonight." Jon breathed a heavy, worried sigh. "Oh," the tape continued, "one last thing: if anyone asks you about what you're doing, you'll act like nothing has happened to you that's out of the ordinary. You will never mention me or that you're under my control. Have fun."

Click. The tape ended.

Without even pausing for a second, Jon put the tape player down and proceeded to hop on his computer (stopping the socked screensaver from happening first), index card in hand. It had been awhile since he moved, but he quickly booked an appointment with a good carrier online. There was no "expedite" option, so he wound up calling them in person to see if this could be done today. Lucky for Mike, they had a free day today, so made it happen. There was a surcharge for such quick turnaround of course, but per Mike's orders, that wasn't an issue for Jon.

Of course, in the back of his head, he was screaming. Even though he put it on a credit card, he couldn't be more in debt. Like, several thousands of dollars in debt. There was absolutely zero things cool about this. He was already struggling month-to-month to pay the rent, but this just added fuel to that terrible fire. He wasn't going to pay off $1000 just like that ... but what other choice did he have? Somehow those fucking socks -- or was it his feet? -- were turning Jon into an obedient little hypno slave, and as it stood, there was nothing he could do about it except move on to the next command, which was ... to mill about and get ready.

Jon had a bit of freedom in this portion but still was amazed that his brain seemed to massage and go over every single word Mike spoke, looking for all possible meanings of each and every phrase. Jon made breakfast, checked his emails -- all the usual. Of course, when he was eating breakfast, all he wanted to do was to dial 911 and beg for help. When he checked his emails, he wanted to send out the biggest SOS the world had ever seen. Yet no, here he was, obedient, his mind frantically trying to figure out what he would do on a regular day until it ran out of options ...

... and when it did, Jon audibly sighed as he got back to the same couch as before, and began removing the clothes he only so recently put on. Now down to his birthday suit, Jon went and felt a slight tingle in his groin when he noticed that pair of socks sitting on the coffee table, taunting him, teasing him. He reached over and grabbed them, held it up to his nose and--

Holy fucking shit. That smell, tangy but somehow fragrant in a notably masculine way, caused Jon's eyes to pop wide open. Hell on fire this got him horny. It's as if his dick suddenly sprung to attention and got harder faster than he had ever experienced. That smell was ... intoxicating. After one whiff, he just couldn't get enough of it. Jon pressed the socks even further into his nostrils and felt that foot funk hit is body faster than any drug he has ever tried. He was high on sock sweat, and fucking loved it. With jackhammer ferocity, Jon grabbed his dick and started wailing on it. *Oh god, this feels so good* his cock said, fighting with his brain in a one-sided competition.

A stupid grin crept across Jon's face, one of pleasure so good it feels like it's draining you of IQ points the harder your cock gets. Each sniff pushed that dominant smell further up his nostrils, the tendrils of it reaching into his brain and seeping into every nook and crevice it could find. Jon felt himself becoming addicted and overwhelmed, but all he could do now was just bring himself to the edge of cumming, cumming harder than he ever had before ... and then he stopped.

His dick was now screaming, demanding to know where this payoff was. It throbbed, it bounced, it swayed, but Jon couldn't do anything: all he could do was just bring himself to the very possible edge per Mike's commands. Jon had never felt so used in his life. He was no longer touching his pulsating erection, even though every fiber of his body was doing all they could to force him to finish stroking -- but no, it was on to the next command. It was Sharpie time.

Standing up and going to the bathroom with marker in hand, precum dripping along the hardwood apartment floor as he did so, Jon faced the mirror and thought really hard about how to write the phrase "I Am a Footslave" on himself backwards. It took a few false starts with the marker, but he finally got the phrase on his forehead, even if he initially thought his "I" was about right only to find out later it was too big, causing the rest of the phrase's letters to get narrower as he ran out of forehead space. He applied it again once to each cheek.

As he was doing this, branding himself some sort of public pervert that in his heart of hearts he knew he wasn't, that abject feeling of humiliation absolutely consumed Jon. As he started writing "I Am a Footslave" across his chest, he couldn't shake the feeling that his body had become nothing but a marionette, Mike the puppetmaster who was *very* amused by the fact that he could control a puppet with such giddiness and glee. Yet as helpless as Jon felt in the moment, even as he was signing himself away, he couldn't shake the fact that against his better wills, pleasure was indeed radiating out of his cock, and it felt fucking phenomenal.

Sure that Mike would be pleased with all the markings now covering his nude, supple body, Jon returned to the couch once more and sniffed the socks just a bit, that hit of pleasure still there, awakening every nerve ending. He edged himself further, then finally turned on the phone. The background image was a drawing of a bare foot. Maybe it was a custom one? If Mike has this power over everyone, commissioning a piece of art would be no problem. These are the only free thoughts Jon can afford himself that aren't Mike's instant-gospel commands.

With his cock being pumped in one hand and the phone in the other, Jon flipped over into the Contacts, and, as Mike promised, there was only one: "Master". Jon started the video call as he edged himself further, each pulse from his cockhead more radiant and even slightly painful than the last.

The call connected. Mike appeared to be in his usual dapper wear, thin gold-rimmed glasses affixed to his face.

"Ah," Mike said, taking one quick glance at what Jon was sure was a never-ending litany of slaves, "so you got my message."

"Pleasssssssse," Jon let out, defeated and deflated, "will you let me cum, sir?" His fapping continued.

"Let me see the writing all over you," Mike replied, ever so matter-of-factly. Jon angled the camera so that Mike could get a full voyeuristic view of the scribblings on his newest piece of slavemeat.

"Let me see that cock," demanded Mike. Jon brought the phone oh so much closer to this throbbing, redder-by-the-second member. The precum glistened in the eye of the phone's camera.

"Very good," Mike said. "Back to your face." Jon held the camera above his head, so he could see the writing and his hardon at the same time. "When will the movers be at your place?"

"About 4," said Jon, still edging himself.

"Good," said Mike. "I'm going to be nice and let you do what you need to before then. You should probably clear some shit out of the way, no? I have some furniture and some computer equipment. Nothing that can't fit into your space already. Set me up in the bigger of the bedrooms there. Once that's done, you can do what you will outside of telling anyone about your current state or contacting anyone about it. Help the movers when they come, OK?"

"OK," said Jon, still edging.

"So Jon," Mike started, "answer me honestly: if you could have sex with one of your male friends, who would it be?"

What the actual fuck. Jon's face grimaced, his teeth locked together as if he was pushing back against a dam that was about to burst. The idea never crossed his mind, although he did certainly have some handsome friends. Some buff ones too. Some with some clean jawlines. Some with some firm butts, too. Fuck, no, he didn't have any opinion on the matter but his mouth had something inside of it. Some name it wanted to spit out. He grit his teeth some more.

"C'mon Jon," said Mike. "Spit it out."

"ATLAN!" Jon screamed.

"Atlan?" asked Mike. "The hell kind of name is that?"

"It's Greek or something," Jon said. "I don't know. Dude's built. DJ. I mean, he is from Greece but I don't know the etymology of the word, ya know?"

"But you'd fuck him if you had the chance?" Mike inquired.

Jon grit his teeth again, but his body refused to let him disobey. "Yes."

"He as cute as you?" asked Mike.

"I mean," started Jon, "he's more buff than me but yeah, he's ... he's easy on the eyes."

"Well I'm taking care of some business right now," started Mike, "so once the movers show up at 4, maybe have Atlan show up around 8pm? No, 9pm. I'll be there around that time too and we'll need some manual labor to help get things to where I want them, OK?"

"OK," said Jon, meekly.

"Is there ... anything else you wanted to ask me for?" asked Mike, wryly.

"I really, really, really need to cum," pleaded Jon. "Please. It's really bad. I haven't gone this long without cumming in ... in a while. I need to, please sir."

"OK, how about this," said Mike. "Take those stinky socks that you love so much 'cos you're a footslave pervert and put them to your nose." Jon did so. "Now say 'I'm a footslave pervert' out loud for me."

Jon hated this, but his body giddily replied: "I'm a footslave pervert."

"Again," ordered Mike. Jon kept wanking. "I'm a footslave pervert!" he exclaimed.

"Again," said Mike. "I'm a footslave pervert!" screamed Jon.

"No dice," deemed Mike. "Sniff the socks and edge yourself for another two hours. No cumming unless I say so."

The video call ended. How abrupt. How rude. How fucking horny could Jon be right now? Very, it turns out. Super fucking horny. He had to cum. He really really had to, but his body is carrying out orders, and even with tears welling up in his sockets knowing just how much pleasure and pain he was about to endure, Jon kept Mike's sweaty workout socks to his nose, some dampness on the fabric, and proceeded to wank away. Over the next two hours, he backed off from the edge no fewer than eight different times. He would fuck the world if he could right now, his boner begging for release.

But as Jon would soon find out, release for him was a long, long ways away.

CHAPTER III: THE FEET OF A FRIEND

The movers shook hands and left. After moving a lot of things around, all of Mike's stuff dominated Jon's apartment. Boxes upon boxes, some small, some that had to be tilted on their sides in order to fit through Jon's doorway. It was about 6pm, and ... Jon had nothing to do. Nothing aside from ensuring that Atlan showed up at about 9. Jon texted him, but, per the previous order of not mentioning anything about his situation, just wondered if he was free tonight. Unfortunately, he was, and sure, he'd be there around 9.

Jon's face turned into a distorted, miserable version of its previous self. He was friends with Atlan, but they hung out only sporadically. He was more of a guy you could have at a bar who would be loud and funny, undoubtedly leaving with a girl (and maybe even *your* girl) by the end of the night. Sometimes he was a bit of an asshole, but mostly he was a fun-loving party dude that took that persona he developed in college and forced it into something applicable in the real world: he had a nice finance job, a nice place, but still could be seen on weekends and sometimes even weeknights having one-too-many drinks in the most glorious of fashions. Jon was upset because ... he didn't want to drag him into this. He didn't want to drag anyone into this -- but he had no choice.

With boxes filling up his apartment and time to spare, Jon went out to grab a burger (first washing his face of writings because there was no specific command about that), still doing his usual routine, casually flipping through Facebook on his phone while his brain was working overtime trying to think of how to get out of this fucked up situation. Every impulse he had -- to punch Mike, to phone cops, to do quite frankly anything -- was overridden by Mike's commands.

Jon was frustrated, not just by his situation or his yet-to-cum hardon, but by how all of this, insane as it was, was really making him think a lot about sex. He had edged himself to a guys toes and made out with Mike's socks for two hours. He confessed which of his friends he found hottest. He had gay friends by the bushel (who doesn't, these days?), but even after all of the girls he went down on, right now it's like his mind -- and his libido -- was being forced down a certain lane, like bumpers were put on the bowling lane. He tried to bounce around and certainly had a *sense* of freedom, but ultimately he was going down a very specific direction whether he liked it or not, hitting all those pins, knocking down all those pillars of what he once knew.

Jon sipped the last of his soda at the sit-down Burgerium. A message shot across his phone "Hey man, I'm here early. You in?" It was Atlan. Jon groaned, upset he lured his friend here under false pretenses. He almost wished he could beg Mike for mercy, to do something to him even worse than what he was doing now in order to save Atlan, but those commands kicked in: he texted back "Just finished a burger -- omw!" Jon checked the time: it was 8:32 PM. Maybe, just maybe, he'd be able to use the time before Mike showed up to do ... something.

Some eight minutes later, he found Atlan waiting outside the front door of the building. "Sorry I got here early -- but also not sorry? Like, fuck you for not being around, right?" joked Atlan. "No, you're right man," said Jon. "I gotta keep fucks like you at bay so you know who's in charge -- it's a power play, dawg." They both snickered at their patented bro-banter. Jon turned the keys to the front and lead him up to the second floor.

As Atlan entered the living room, he was a bit gobsmacked by the sheer number of boxes. "Um ... are you moving, dude?" "No," replied Jon. "I ... I got a roommate."

"Oh weird, weren't you like looking for one like ... yesterday?"

Jon grimaced a bit as he wanted to tell the truth but was overridden once again. "I mean, yeah, but this guy was Johnny-on-the-spot and was ready to move in a jiffy."

"Jiffy. Nice," snorted Atlan. "Well, is he here?"

Jon had a nervous face twitch kick in for a half-second. "No, but he'll be back any minute. You'll get to meet him."

"Nice," remarked Atlan. A moment passed in silence. "Is something wrong with you, dude?"

"Yeah," said Jon, his face cracking and his mask of sanity about to slip, seconds before Mike's commands again overrode his source code, "... why aren't you drinking yet?"

"Pfft, 'cos you haven't beer'd me, bro!" shouted Atlan, making his way to the kitchen.

Jon remained calm despite wanting desperately tell Atlan something was wrong. He nervously checked the clock on his phone, fearing that Mike would come home any second.

"Wanna take a walk outside?" Jon spat out, a phrase which didn't violate Mike's commands and still kept within his regular routine.

"Um, why dude?" asked Atlan, popping the cap off of his beer. "We just got some brews."

"I mean, I know," stuttered Jon, it's just that ...

"Dude," interjected Atlan, "you OK? You've been acting all sorts of weird ever since I got here. Everything alright?"

"I mean--" started Jon.

"Out with it!"

A brief, tense air filled the room, but the silence between the boys soon was replaced with the sounds of creaking stairs, as if someone was making their way up to the apartment. Jon's heart raced. The feet reached the second-floor landing and soon made their way to his door. It opened, a bit squeaky.

"Honey, I'm home!" Mike bellowed, entering in that same fancy suit and dress shoes as before, this time carrying a briefcase with him. Jon, gazing as his mental captor at that moment, had never felt so defeated in his life.

"Oh," said Atlan, a bit surprised. "Guess like I'll meet him sooner than thought."

Atlan went to go into the other room, while Jon marinated in his misery. He followed Atlan slowly, knowing full well he was going to be unable to stop what happened next.

Jon turned the corner: the two shook hands. "I'm Mike. You must be Atlan."

"Oh hell yeah," said Atlan. "Jonny Boy here already tell you about me?

"He mentioned you might be stopping by at some point," noted Mike. "I'm glad I got to meet my new roomie's buddies."

Jon noticed that Mike was wearing the same dark-purple suit he wore last night. It didn't look worn at all; in fact, it looked freshly pressed. Jon guessed he either had service done last night on the suit or ... he just has a bunch of 'em.

"Would you mind getting me a beer, Atlan?" asked Mike, again sitting down on the couch where he first started his rule over Jon's life last night. "Sure thing, man," was the response. Atlan left the room and Jon was left standing and staring at Mike, beer in hand, somber and submissive. Mike glanced at him and smirked. "Wait 'til you get a load of this," he said quietly, teasing Jon even further.

Atlan came back with the beverage and handed it to Mike. "Thanks, son," he said. "Now Atlan, how did you meet Jonny here?"

"Oh, ya know," started Atlan, setting himself down on one of the comforters not blocked by Mike's moving boxes in the living room, "we had a lot of classes together. He was into preppy-nerdy shit and I was livin' that sweet frat life. He joined up for Ultimate a few times. We've had more than a few nights of drinking that neither of us could remember -- you know how it is.

"Heh," smirked Mike, "I do."

"How about you?" queried Atlan. "You just move the city or what?"

"Did it ever bother you that Jon's got a foot fetish?" asked Mike, barreling past the question he was just asked.

Atlan arched his eyebrow. "Um, what do you mean?"

"Jon, remind me," started Mike, "what were you doing before you passed out last night?"

Jon's face blushed. Every electrical impulse in his brain went to his mouth, telling it to not move and to--

"Remember, you can't *wait* to tell your friend," added Mike, turning the question into a new command.

A smile was forced upon Jon's face. "Oh, I was just edging myself to the shape of your toes in sheer socks," said Jon in a casual, loving tone. "It was so great. I only wish I got to cum."

Atlan wasn't so much shocked by this as he was just very, very confused. "Um ... what?"

"You didn't know this?" asked Mike, playing a part.

"No, I didn't know ... that at all," said Atlan, his voice still tentative.

"Oh that's weird," Mike said. "It was one of the first things he told me. Must've been conditional to me getting the place. I'm fine with it though, 'cos, like, who doesn't love getting a good footrub at the end of the day, ya know?"

"I mean ..." started Atlan.

"Well, here, let me show you," stated Mike, setting his dress shoe'd feet up on the coffee table in front of him. "Jon, why don't you be a good boy and crawl on all fours to my feet, trying to take my shoes off with your teeth?"

"No way," started Atlas, but he cut himself short as he saw his buddy kneel the ground, set the beer he was holding on the floor, and crawl in his white t-shirt and light blue jeans on the floor over to the coffee table where Mike's feet were propped up. As his face approached the bottom of the shoe soles, Jon stood up on his knees, put his hands on either side of Mike's feet, and arched his head in, trying to line up his teeth with the end of the shoelace that Mike had tied so lovingly into a knot. The laces fell to either side of the shoe, and Jon then did what he could to put his teeth between the back of the shoe and Mike's ankle, looking for leverage in a bid to try and wedge them off. There wasn't a lot of space to maneuver, so Jon whimpered a bit with difficulty. Mike started snickering.

"You ever seen anything like this, Atlan?" asked Mike as he took a swig from his beer.

"Um ... no," stated Atlan, his jaw still agape. "I ... Jon, are you gay?"

"No," said Mike on Jon's behalf, "he's just an object right now. He'll learn to love his new obsession very soon. In fact, you can use your hands now, Jon. Get both of my shoes off."

Jon undid the laces of the other shoe and slid both dress shoes off, again revealing Mike's massive toes stretching and spreading within the constraints of the thick sheer fabric. Jon stared at them, but his held tilted lower, dragged down by shame.

Unsure what psycho-sexual mindgames were going on, Atlan was ready to move. "Well," he started, putting his beer down, "I ... uh ... I think I'll let you two do what you need to do and I'm gonna head--"

"Stop!" Mike commanded. Atlan did so. *Fuck*, thought Jon, *he's got Atlan now*. "Atlan, you're going to stay here for a good portion of the night and you're already looking forward to it."

Without even a hint or break in the moment, Atlan's face burst into a large smile. "You're right," he said, stoked and zombified in equal measure. "I'm so ready for whatever's about to happen next, Mike!"

"Good boy," Mike said, his socked feet stretching and flexing. "You can't stop staring at my feet, can you?"

"No," Atlan said, "I can't!"

"They're so hypnotic, aren't they?"

"They are!" said Atlan.

"They ... excite you, sexually."

Atlan's face twinged a bit but that smile morphed into a horny little sneer. "Yeah, they're pretty great."

"You could even maybe turned on by them, right?" asked Mike, coyly.

"Yeah," Atlan leered a bit.

"Why don't you touch yourself through your pants, Atlan?" The Greek boy immediately proceeded to do so.

"You should start looking at my feet with feasting eyes as well, Jon," commanded Mike. Jon's head swiveled towards the sheer gods in agreement. Jon immediately began touching himself while on his knees.

"Atlan, join him on the floor," Mike ordered. Atlan also kneeled, both boys fondling themselves while staring at their master's toes bend and stretch in that thin, sultry fabric.

"OK, boys," started Mike. "Lean in and sniff while you jack yourselves."

Both submissive men immediately undid their buckles and pulled their pants down their thighs a little bit, freeing their cocks as they pressed their faces into the stink of Mike's socked soles. They both took heavy inhales, Mike's pheromones slipping into their nostrils and up to their skulls, impregnating their brains with thoughts of obedience and subservience. The more they sniffed, the harder they got.

"Boys, are you turned on by the smell of my feet?" Mike asked in a devilish tone.

"Yes," the boys both moaned, their noses still burrowing into Mike's toes.

"Well, just wait until you both take my socks off. In fact, you should do that now," Mike commanded.

Ravenously, both guys reached up Mike's legs and each grabbed their own sock rim, pulling it down and off as quickly as possible, soon exposing dominant, powerful, meaty size 14 bare soles and toes in full view.

"Now just kneel there and edge yourself while you stare at my foot flesh," cooed Mike.

They where were: perfect. Masculine, dominant, large, beautiful. Pale in the richest of ways, the tips of those toes radiating the color pink, as if begging to be sucked on. The wide ball of the foot, the range of motion the toes possessed, all of it: it was incredible. It was the most glorious sight to look at. Jon was genuinely hard, genuinely turned on by such a visage. He ... he wanted to touch them. He couldn't believe himself, but--

"Fuck your feet are gorgeous!" exclaimed Atlan out of nowhere.

"I know," stated Mike. "It's not that both of you are under their spell of attractiveness, it's that both of you *want* to be under the spell of my godly bare feet."

"Yes!" they both exclaimed, their jacking getting faster.

"Neither of you cum though: just edge yourselves stupid."

Jon couldn't recall a time when his rod was ever this rigid, those spare nanoseconds before each stroke radiating a horniness which was beyond anything he could understand. He was fucking *hard* for Mike's feet, and he couldn't rationally believe that here his buddy was right next to him, wanking hard on that foot-driven erection as he shoved his face into Mike's big bare feet. Jon kept looking at Atlan, hoping their eyes would connect, hoping he'd see some sort of "we're in this together" kind of connection -- but no, he was lost in lust, smiling and moaning and his mouth turning into aches of pleasure as he kept on going down this road he had no control over. In an instant, he was lost, maybe forever.

"OK, boys, that's enough," commanded their new unshod emperor.

"Strip down to your socks and boxers," Mike commanded.

They both did so, eager, compliant. Both slaves clearly spent time at the gym at their own volition, but Jon couldn't recall if he ever saw Atlan shirtless before: fine skin stretched over ribs and worked-on muscles, that light olive tinge to his pigment doing nothing but highlighting his most desirable attributes. Jon's eyes couldn't help but wander though, drawing down to Atlan's cock, still sticking straight out with his powder-blue briefs bunched up right under them.

"You can pull your underwear back up over your pulsating erections, boys," Mike commanded.

They both did so, but Jon was wearing briefs, and so in sliding them back up, his cock ended up sticking out of the two folds of fabric at the front of every pair of briefs. It was still exposed.

"Looks like someone just can't contain his excitement, can he?" joked Mike. Atlan's eyes fell down to see Jon's vibrant erection sticking out of those boxers, himself grinning.

"Hmm," mused Mike. "There is some fun we can have here before we get you both set to work. Jon, clasp your arms over your head." Jon did so, still facing the endtable where Mike's feet were sticking out. "Atlan, why don't you stand behind our boy, like ... really close."

"You got it, sir!" said Atlan, more than happy to follow through with another command. He stood directly behind his friend, the tent in his boxers more than snuggly tracing the boxer-covered curves of Jon's tight ass. "We're very snug, sir!" shouted Atlan, an excited and horny little puppy.

"Good," said Mike. "Jon, is your ass clean? Like, relatively."

"Uh, yeah," said Jon, his eyebrows arching with questions as the stress of keeping his arms clasped over his head started to get to him.

"Good," said Mike once more, a sly grin sneaking onto his own face. "Now Jon, I figured you guys are already horny enough -- what's a little more? Jon, you can't move your arms no matter what. You can just stare at my bare soles and admire how horny they make you feel."

Jon already felt that unwilling electrical storm start to form in his loins as he stared.

"Now Atlan," started Mike, "please reach around your friend's front and lightly tease and play with his nipples as he stares at my dominant feet."

"No!" shouted Jon, involuntarily. "Shut up," said Mike, to which Jon did so, even with his face still a bit panicked.

He felt it. That first flick, every tiny ridge of Atlan's fingerprint slowly rubbing up against the tip of his nipple, the bit of dull fingernail edge scraping against his sensitive areolas, each second of touching instantly sending a signal to his already-embarrassed erection to get hornier. And hornier. And hornier. Both hands were now in position, and fingers were dancing, twerking, flicking, and playing with his sensitive skin. His cock immediately started bouncing and dripping, his cockhead turning into a little precum factor as all he did was stare at Mike's bare feet, that big toe just begging to be sucked on. Flick flick flick went Atlan's fingers, and being unable to put his arms down and fend off the erotic attack, Jon's cock twitched and bounced and absolutely throbbed that deep kind of throb that you can feel through your whole body.

"Fuck, I'm gonna cum!" shouted Jon.

"Stop," instructed Mike, to which Atlan immediately refrained from further nippleplay. Jon, arms still up, was breathing heavily, feeling like his erection was about to pop. It was so close. He felt he was one brainwave, one electric impulse away from shooting out giant screaming rockets of hot liquid seed. Each passing second of it not happening weighed on him, sending him into a state of genuine sadness, his arms tired, his body now rigid and sensitive and fraught with anticipation, all of it ebbing out of him, slowly.

"Jon, pull your boxers off," instructed Mike, toes curling a bit. Jon did so, pulling the elastic around his waist and letting the fabric fall to the floor, his dick still hard all this time.

"Good boy. Now Atlan, please proceed to rim Jon."

"What?" said Atlan, confused. Jon's eyebrows perked up.

"You heard me: put your face in your friend's ass and lick his sensitive pink asshole," Mike stated, firmly. "Oh, and enjoy it."

Jon opened his mouth to say something when he suddenly felt Atlan's hands grab each of his butt cheeks and a felt his friend's warm tongue slide its way across his asshole, causing Jon to gasp. Mike laughed at this and curled his toes on more time. Jon's mouth stood agape as sensations of pleasure began shooting up through his anus, that warm, wet tongue playing with his body and proving whole new realms of pleasure for him, at times absolutely overwhelming. Unable to fend off the attack, Jon just stood there, naked and hard, the tongue searching for a pleasure button inside of his asshole as his new master looked on, enjoying the sight of Jon's still-hard boner occasionally twitching, unsure of what to make of this explosive amount of sensation.

"Kneel on all fours," Mike commanded, and Jon did so, his tired arms holding him up as he kneeled like a dog, his face now mere inches away from Mike's feet. Atlan joined behind, his command to rim his friend and enjoy it still being fresh in his mind, the kneeling Jon suddenly making his butt that much more open and accessible for Atlan's eager, hungry tongue. Being this close to Mike's feet caused Jon to panic a bit, as from here the smell was so powerful, it made him feel more helpless than ever before. Mike knew this and enjoyed it.

"Do you like being rimmed while being this close to my beautiful bare feet, boy?"

"Yes," moaned Jon, Atlan's tongue working him like a puppet.

"Good. Do you like being used like the pleasure toy that you are?" asked Mike.

Atlan dove deeper than before. "YES!" screamed Jon, too awash in pleasure to protest.

"Good," said Mike. "Now why don't you give my feet some thank-you licks to show your appreciation."

Without even hesitating, Jon stuck out his tongue and began lapping at Mike's heels and lower sole, lapping and lapping and licking and licking that sweet-salty flavor off of his master's bare paws. Jon had never tasted a foot before, but there was something beguiling and hypnotic about the flavor, something that he couldn't quite put a finger on but something that made him crave it all the more.

"With each lick, you love male bare feet all the more," Mike commanded. Jon tried nodding his head while in the act of licking.

"With each lick, you get more and more turned on by the idea of being used as a pleasure slave for men, giving up your orgasms to instead make sure other men achieve theirs," Mike commanded. Jon kept licking, his neck growing tired with the repetitive notion but not being in a place to complain, doubly so when the sensations that

Atlan's tongue was giving his ass were by no means growing stale.

"OK, you can both stop," Mike ordered. The boys stood up to a kneel, both tired from the aggressive, non-stop sexual acts they just committed.

"Atlan, how was that for you?" Mike inquired.

"Oh, it was ... it was different," said the exhausted Greek boy.

"What was your favorite part?" Mike probed.

"Uhh," thought Atlan, genuinely unsure of what to say but compelled to tell the truth under Mike's hypnotic commands, "probably hearing Jon moan, to be honest."

"Good," said Mike. "Now go wash up your face real good and come back." Atlan stood up and walked to the bathroom.

"Now, Jon," Mike started, "you really want to cum, don't you?"

"Yes sir," Jon panted.

"Now, if you had your druthers, how would you go about doing that?"

Jon's brain raced. Previously it was so easy: eating a girl out, some general fucking, maybe sucking on her toes, whathaveyou ... but these concepts, while still in his head, were foggier, dulled in hue, a bit out of reach. These were things that in his bones he knew he liked but, maybe, just not as much right now. Instead, all that was floating to the forefront of his mind was his the shape of Mike's toes. The color of the bottoms of those soles, the folds and creases that he could see when the toes were clenched. It was a glorious sight to see, and one that he wanted to see more.

"I want to suck on your toes," Jon said, surprising even himself.

The corner or Mike's mouth lifted upwards. He was pleased with this response. "Good boy."

Atlan came back, still a bit sweaty but still clean.

"Alright," started Mike, opening up his briefcase and pulling something out. "First off, both of you find your phones and give them to me with your lockscreen passwords disabled." Atlan had to think for a moment where his phone was but Jon started walking to where he saw it last, both boys' bare feet making soft slapping sounds on the apartment hardwood as they milled about. They came back to Mike's attention and fidgeted with the settings before both handed him their smartphones, awash with too much personal data to even fathom.

"Good," said Mike again, pulling his feet from their reclined position on the coffee table to a now sitting position. He slid a piece of paper over to them. "Hope you both ate well. This is a crude map I had another slave do of your place when I described it from memory. I had him also indicate where each of the items I moved in with should go. Obviously, Jon, I will take the larger of your bedrooms here. You can keep yours, but you'll thank me later for such generosity."

"Understood," said Jon, accepting his fate reluctantly. "So now, you are each to open up all my stuff and get this all ready and looking nice by tomorrow morning, OK?"

"Yes sir," the boys said in almost-unison.

"But before we begin," Mike said, holding up a finger, "Atlan, look at Jon's naked body and tell me how sexy it is."

Atlan turned to his pale-skinned friend and eyed him up and down. It was weird: Jon never felt in his life that he had been ogled in such a fashion.

"He's really good-lookin'," said Atlan. "Can't say I ever noticed it before."

"I know, right?" said Mike. "And doesn't he just look great when he's in service to a man, like when you saw him sniffing my socks earlier?"

"Uh, yeah," said Atlan, having never fully digested that concepts as something to be considered "hot" by any means. "Yeah, I guess so."

"Well, Atlan, you guys are going to get me set up by the morning, but you're also going to make sure you take breaks and have some fun while you do so. I'm going to enslave Jon to you. He's going to do your bidding. While you both work together to unbox my things and set up my bed and computer all according to this diagram, feel free to use Jon however you see fit. Want him to suck *your* toes? Say the word. Make him sniff your crotch. Have him swallow your cock all the way down to the fucking hilt. Lick your fingers. Whatever you want to explore during sexual interactions with a man, Jon is here to do it for you. And Jon, you'll give yourself over to him and gladly allow yourself to be the piece of pleasuremeat that you are. Understood?"

"Yes sir," both guys said.

"Try it out, Atlan," Mike encouraged.

"Uhh, how?" the Greek asked.

"Atlan, listen to me closely," Mike said, leaning forward a bit. "You are strong. You are confident. You are fucking sexy. You have someone who is here to please you. He's here to indulge your fantasies, to suck up your sweat, to make you feel like you can do anything. Go easy. Think about something degrading and hot."

Atlan searched his mind, and a sly, confident smirk emerged out of him. He lifted up his arm and looked right at Jon.

"Lick my pit," he commanded.

Jon arched his neck around so he was just under Atlan's armpit and proceed to lick that cavernous arm bend, a good amount of sweat in there from the sexual adventures earlier but nothing too overpowering. Jon, obedient servant that he was, did long laps with his tongue from right under the armpit up to the underside of Atlan's bicep. His face was covered in Atlan's stink, and Atlan laughed a bit: the sensation certainly did tickle a bit, but he was rather enjoying seeing his friend lapping up his armpit like it was a giant slab of candy.

"OK, stop," Atlan said. "This is going to be *fun!*" he exclaimed.

"Damn right," said Mike. "Now you boys get to work. I'm going to go through your phones and find some fun stuff on them I'm sure. Jon, I'll be going home for tonight but I expect my new bed -- here in my new home -- to be ready by morning. You boys better be ready for whenever I get here."

"Yes sir," they said. Mike stood up and put his shoes and socks on -- much to the chagrin of the hard, toe-obsessed slave boys. Mike made his exit through the front door of the apartment as the nude boys immediately bent over and sniffed the part of the hardwood where his bare soles touched last. They then looked up at all the boxes the movers brought.

"Oh, and Atlan," Mike said, opening the front door once more, "Make Jon tell you any embarrassing story you want to know. Nothing is off limits. Have fun with his humiliation. Oh -- and make sure he doesn't cum."

Jon looked up at his friend but saw the virus had taken over: Atlan was really going to enjoy the next few hours of close bonding with his buddy.

CHAPTER IV: ASSEMBLING THE COURT

Mike was being roused from his sleep by the best kind of alarm clock: a slave's tongue dragging across his soles.

While groggy at first, Mike's other foot tried to subconsciously shake the sensation off, but seconds later the tongue was back, slurping up the flavor of his godfeet and rousing him out of a sleep. That tongue was hungry, thirsting, clearly trying to lap up as much of the taste as he could. "Stop," Mike had to shout, to which the tongue immediately retracted. Still only half-assembling his thoughts, Mike lifted himself out of bed and dangled his legs off of the side. A pair of hands slid his favorite, comfiest pair of flip-flops into place, allowing him to slip into them with ease.

Once that toepost was properly gripped, his bed slave simply kneeled, awaiting further command. The slave was wearing only a pair of briefs and was deep in Mike's control. The slapping sounds of the sandals echoed against the walls of Mike's room, Mike leaving and not even asking his bed slave to join him. This was to be expected: Mike rarely allowed his bed slave outside of the bedroom, but the amount of personal time he spent with Mike's toes was enough to satisfy him throughout the day.

Mike's house was populated with slaves, and they had been programmed to follow a very specific routine when he was not around. They cooked, cleaned, went on grocery runs, and did webcam shows in a small area set up in the living room that proved to be very popular -- Mike had trained them well. They had do's and don't's that they had to follow at all times, but the biggest rule was prepping for whenever Mike was home. They made themselves as clean as possible and continued to make sure his life was easy as it could be upon his return. The slaves could be "themselves" when they were just around each other, but they never got to cum unless expressly ordered by Mike. However, since he was usually exhausted when he got home, he'd have little time to take care of their needs, even if some of them had gone weeks without orgasm.

As Mike walked to the kitchen all flopped and handsome, a breakfast of freshly-made eggs benedict was waiting for him. A glass of OJ, a glass of milk, a coffee with two creams in it. Sometimes Mike would take only a sip from one of the glasses before leaving but sometimes he'd devour all three. Regardless, all were available to him every morning, fresh for whenever he wakes up.

Cooking for him every morning was Dan, a nerdy, plainfaced, buzzcut man in his mid-20s who slaved over meals with precision, using whatever leftovers he had from making Mike's meals to create meals for the rest of the house slaves. Through trials and failures (and a good dose of humiliation for whenever he got a meal "wrong" in Mike's views), Dan was able to create good meals down to a science. Naked save for an apron (which nonetheless did a poor job of concealing his hardon every time Mike walked into the room), Dan's desire was the same as everyone else's in the house: to serve Mike and his Masterful godfeet.

At a desk nearby was Brian, a thin, sandal-loving bro who had a knack for all things electronic. He had short brown hair and a sly grin, but was mainly responsible for all things tech, from maintaining the jerkoff-for-cash website that Mike had set up as well as converting livestreamed videos into other, purchasable formats for their digital customers. He was also responsible for setting up any and all tech in Mike's apartment, as well as doing any smartphone jailbreaking that was needed when Mike wanted to bring a new slave into the fold. He was going through Jon and Atlan's contacts right then and there as Mike was sitting at the breakfast counter, eating his wonderfully cooked meal.

Also in attendance was Patrick, the pretty, boyish one. A bit beefier than Dan, Patrick was in his early 30s but still had a boyish face, making him the most popular star of Mike's online webcam show empire. Every role in the house had its own perk to it, and while the bed slave (a wisp of an early-20s boy named Nathan) got to spend the most quality time with Mike's bare soles, Patrick at the very least got to jerk off on camera, cumming at least two or three times a day. However, that meant that he must always be kept horny and must always perform as needed, meaning that even if Mike makes him cum once or twice before a show, he still had to give the customers full-bore, moaning cumshots, no matter the cost. Sometimes he truly was a cum-dribbling workhorse.

While Atlan and Jon continued to unpack all of Mike's things at his new lair, those boys were not clued into the source of Mike's powers like the houseslaves were. No, these well-trained boys knew the secret to Mike's powers: the pheromones given off by his feet.

Mike never discussed it, but as far as the slaves could tell, anyone that's exposed to the pheromones had no choice but to accept Mike's spoken words as gospel. If he said you were turned on to something, you were. If he told you to do pushups for an hour, even if your body screams for mercy, you'd have to. The extent of his power was total, and anyone that sniffed his feet, socks, or shoes would be invigorated all over again.

Yet that sniffing was a constant. The slaves learned that if one doesn't "re-up" on his pheromones after 12 hours, the effects would start to wear off, and for a select few, the effect was immediate.

This happened to Patrick once. Mike was pretty good about returning home before 12 hours was up, but one time, he was really cutting it close. The slaves had done their chores, the video sessions were filmed for the day, and Dan, Patrick, and Brian looked at each other, nervous. After being under Mike's control for so long (in fact, it was so constant that all of them had basically forgotten about how the passage of time works -- but they knew they had been enslaved for at *least* a year), they were unsure what to do if the effects of his scent ever wore off. They had gotten so used to serving a devious man who was their sexual everything that they almost weren't sure if they were ready to "go back" to a normal life. Besides, what's normal when you've been living as a foothorny sex slave for so long?

"He's coming up the stairs," Nathan called out from the bedroom on that fateful day, the boys still standing, nervous. Patrick's mind, however, was ferocious in its intensity. He needed to get out. He needed to be free. Although he was just in socks and a tight thong, he was ready to bolt out the front door. He tried willing his body to move. It didn't take. He tried again. No go. Now even he could hear Mike's footsteps go up the back alley stairs leading up to the apartment. He willed himself one more time -- and his body moved.

He ran towards the front door, opened it and dashed right as Mike walked in. Mike looked at a clearly-worried Dan and Brian, his pheromones again filling up the room.

"Patrick?" he asked. Both slaves nodded. "OK," Mike said. "This won't take long. Here's what you do ..."

Patrick was dashing through city alleys and main streets, his ass mostly hanging out of his thong but himself not really caring. He sprinted with vigor, not knowing where he was going but just trying to get far away. While Mike certainly allowed the boys to do day trips under his supervision, he had been locked inside that eternal pleasure cove of Mike's mind for so long that he had basically lost all sense of direction. It was dusk out, so there were still people milling about, many giving him looks for his noted state of undress. The air was chill, but he didn't care, running in a panic; running because he could finally run on his own volition at long last.

He eventually made his way to a bus station that was fairly underused. He had no money to speak of, but took a moment and sat down on a bench on the inside terminal, plexiglass separating him from a view of the streets. He sat down, exhausted from running, and just thought for a moment. Thought his own thoughts, even if they were panicked ones. It was nice though -- those barriers in and restrictions that had been placed in his brain were finally removed. He felt a bit of freedom. It was great. It was refreshing, even as his lungs continued to breathe in and out in rapid succession.

As he sat there, calming down, only the occasional person would walk by. Even in a thong and some black socks, few really took a glance at him: they had seen more than enough craziness on city public transit that this was just another sight to shove into their peripherals. Patrick leaned over to put his face in his hands, and did all that he could to think. He tried to remember where he lived prior to this. Was it an apartment? Yes, it had to be. Did he have a roommate? He felt like that was the case. Unless he lived alone. Did he live alone? His mind was racing. He tried thinking of phone numbers, but couldn't remember one, his reliance on his cell phone was something he was just now taking for granted. Mike made him turn in his phone when he was captured, only to later have it mined for horrendously personal details. Maybe he could rummage for coins on the floor and try to find a payphone. Who would he call though? Maybe the police to report this maniac. But what's the point if Mike could just take his socks off in an interrogation room and have a police officer let him go? What if he turned every officer there into a tool whose only purpose was to look for him? What if--

"Hello, Patrick," said a deep-but-thin voice. Patrick recognized it. He looked up. It was Nathan, the bed slave.

Patrick didn't see a lot of Nathan back at the place but recognized his threadbare frame and nerdy face. Even more unusual was the fact that Nathan was wearing clothes: jeans, a button-down shirt, brown shoes, glasses. He looked nice. Normal.

"Holy fuck, did you make it out too?!" cried Patrick. Nathan was very casual in his mannerisms as he sat down next to the mostly-naked panic man.

"Well, I'm sitting here next to you, aren't I?"

Patrick embraced Nathan and started sobbing into his chest. "Goodness," he cried, "I can't believe we did it. I think we're far enough away now. Where did you get those clothes? Are those Mike's? Are they yours? Was there a stash in the bedroom I didn't know about? Was--"

"Patrick, Patrick, Patrick, my boy," said Nathan very matter-of-factly. "There is no need to worry about those things. You're going to be OK."

"What a relief," sighed Patrick.

"You're going home," said Nathan, reaching into one of his pockets.

"Thank god."

"Here, I brought you a memento from it ..." said Nathan, holding up a piece of cloth in front of Patrick's face.

Patrick looked at it for a good 10 seconds before all the blood drained out of his face, rendering him pale with horror.

"Oh no," exclaimed Patrick, his hands trying to cover up his nose and mouth. Even one molecule was enough to do him in, but maybe -- just maybe -- he had gotten lucky.

"Yes," said Nathan, then pulling out a phone. He opened it up, pressed a button, and had someone on the line in an instant.

"I got him," Nathan said. He nodded his head. "Patrick, this is for you ..." he said as he handed the phone over.

With his nose and mouth still covered, Patrick continued to shake his head no, but Nathan inched the phone closer to Patrick's ear. Patrick closed his eyes as if that somehow would shield him from what was about to happen, but then he heard Mike's voice:

"Sniff the sock, Patrick."

In an instant, he reached out for the sock in Nathan's hand and brought it to his nostrils. He took a deep inhale. He felt those walls and barriers lock into place in his mind. He was trapped again. Locked again. Helpless again. He was a bit surprised that even without Mike being physically present, his voice was still so tightly tied into the condition of his brain that all it took was one sniff of his socks to bring him back into the fold. Patrick had never felt so defeated in his life.

"He good, Nate?" asked Mike over the phone.

"He's back, sir," Nathan replied. By this time Patrick figured out that Mike had put the boys in regular clothes and had them fan out over the city to look for him. He was a bit surprised he was found so quickly but also realized that he truly hadn't gotten all that far. Patrick really resented Nathan, but also knew that he was under controlled orders, just as he was soon to be.

"Patrick, why don't you sniff the socks proudly as you go home, saying 'I'm sorry, I'm a footslave' out loud so any passerbys may notice. No rush to get home, now that you're under, by the way," ordered Mike.

"Yes, sir," said Patrick, broken. The call ended. Nathan stood up with Patrick and started walking with him back home, Patrick starting to feel a bit cold in his thong and wet, dirty socks, but nonetheless walking with Mike's socks directly in his nostrils. "I'm sorry, I'm a footslave!" Patrick shouted as Nathan shuffled along with him, guiding him back to the apartment that Mike had turned into a lair.

It took the boys an hour to get home, but when Patrick walked up the back alley stairs and made his way to the door, he opened it only to find his fellow slaves waiting for him, naked and hard. Dan and Brian stood there, gorgeous, giving a few quick pumps to their cocks and then letting go, waiting several seconds, then doing a few quick pumps again. Clearly, the boys had been prepped to edge in anticipation of Patrick's return. Patrick briefly scanned their faces: there was the carnal lust in their eyes bred by months upon months of Mike's commands, but there was also a lilt of crushing disappointment behind their glances, sad that even in a mad break, one of them wasn't able to escape.

"Well, well, well," uttered Mike, stepping into view, fully suited save any footwear, "it appears that the prodigal son has returned."

"I'm sorry, I'm a footslave," Patrick uttered for the umpteenth time.

"You can stop that," said Mike. "Lose the socks. Dan, get him a water. All that running must have taken a lot out of him."

Everyone knew that as devious as Mike was, he had a low tolerance for dirty, filthy things, so socks as ruined as Patrick's right now would have to be disposed of. Patrick removed them and placed them in a garbage can in the kitchen. (He took off his thong as well, seeing everyone already fully naked.) He knew he'd be scrubbing the parts where he walked in before too long. Dan, still hard, handed Patrick a water bottle, which he devoured ravenously.

"Good boy," Mike uttered. "Now listen up everyone: today's little escape attempt was bound to happen. I blame myself, for not holding myself to strict enough a standard and coming home in time. However, there's going to be some changes tomorrow. I'm going to have you guys start hanging up my smelliest socks in corners of the house to maximize the smell. Dan, every six hours you'll take a pair, spray them with a bit of water, put them in a bag in the microwave for about 20 seconds, and hang them out here again so that way my scent is a constant gift to you all. Got it?"

"Yes, sir," said Dan, obediently.

"Now as for our little runaway ... well, we'll all have to dissuade him of such notions again. Brain, how many video sessions did our friend have today?"

"He came twice, sir," said Brian, bluntly.

"Good," said Mike, soon pulling out two chairs from the kitchen counter. He placed one in front of the other, then sat in one and used the other as a footrest, letting his massive bare feet hang off of the edge. Everyone stood there in awe (including a now-nude Nathan from the doorway of the bedroom). Those massive monsters looked so veiny and powerful and masculine and dominant. All were transfixed, including, begrudgingly, Patrick.

"Patrick, my boy," said Mike, teasingly, "do ... do you like what you see?"

The pheromones were in, as was the fix. Patrick didn't want to, but couldn't not stare at Mike's bare soles and especially those long, plump toes of his. He felt that electricity in his groin and knew there was no going back. He was getting hard. No, he was hard. He was *extremely* hard. Fuck.

"Sir, may I please touch my cock?" Patrick asked, meekly.

"No," Mike said. "You may drag your cock on the edges of my toes, however."

Instantly Patrick moved over to the dangling feet of his master and, without touching it with his hands, dragged his cock across the tips of Mike's toes as if tracing them onto paper. The sensation of those toeprints against his too-sensitive, already-dripping red cockhead was almost too much.

"Sir, can I please cum?" Patrick begged, still unable to put his hand on his rod, which was driving him batty.

"No," said Mike. "Keep tracing."

The more Patrick did it, the more his foot-addicted dick got harder, longer, wetter. The veins were absolutely protruding out on his shaft, but there he was, dragging his meat across the tips of Mike's toes, feeling full barefoot sensations, and fuck, it was bliss. He *desperately* wanted to just fuck Mike's feet then and there but knew he couldn't. All he could do was make contact with those toes over and over again. And then again. His dick was even more sensitive. Then again. He was stuck on a loop. A loop of torment. Those dry toes making contact with the stream of pre coming out of his cock, glistening, making his lust for feet amplified all the more. Christ, his dick was touching Mike's feet. HIS DICK WAS ON MIKE'S FEET.

"SIR, I'M GONNA CUM!" Patrick shouted.

"Keep tracing," Mike said, dryly. It was too late, one more contact with the long perfect toes was all Patrick's cock needed to explode, and boy it did, Patrick gasping as his dick pulsed and pulsed and pulsed, rockets of cum shooting out over Mike's toes and the pants of his fine suit. He came and came and came until it felt like there was nothing left.

Patrick looked up at Mike, humiliated and pleasured and dumbfounded, as Mike simply stood up and put the chairs back to their setting at the kitchen counter. He took off his pants to reveal those gloriously hairy legs and a nice pair of blue boxer-briefs. He held the pants up in his hand.

"Nathan, make sure these are cleaned properly," he said, the hard bed slave emerging from the doorway to grab the pants before retreating back inside.

"Dan, get out the video camera," Mike ordered. Dan, still hard, proceeded to do so.

"Now Patrick," Mike started, "if I'm not mistaken, you're really ticklish, aren't you?"

"Yes," Patrick confessed, mortified by whatever words were going to come next.

"Good," said Mike. "Now here's the thing: when you escape from my presence, that's not a good thing, so I'm going to make not-good things happen to you, OK?"

"Yes sir," Patrick submitted.

"You are enslaved to the rest of the boys until they've filmed you doing a dry shot."

"I'm sorry sir," started Brian, tending to his own raging hardon. "What do you mean?"

"Oh, it's simple," said Mike, heading to bed. "Tickle the fucker until he can't breathe. Then restrain him and use that raging foot fetish of his to get him hard. Tease and tickle him until he cums. Film it. Then tickle him for another half hour. Then tie him down and tease him until he cums again. Keep doing it, even as he begs you to stop. Do and film every load he shoots. I want to see the anguish in his eyes. Who knows: we might sell this on the site. Keep him cumming until all the cum is drained out of his balls and he starts shooting blanks. Once you've captured him shooting blanks on film, you all can go sleep. Got it?"

"Yes sir," the boys all said in unison.

"Oh, and boys," Mike said, about to enter his bedroom, "only Patrick can cum during this little session. If that frustrates you sexually 'cos you haven't cum in a week -- please feel free to take it out on the boy who escaped. Maybe get him to dry shoot a second time. Up to you. Have fun."

Mike closed the door.

What followed was over seven hours of some of the most merciless erotic torment ever inflicted on a human, with the raging, insatiable footboners of Brian, Dan, and Nathan driving a cruel streak through them, forcing them to really make sure all of Patrick's tickle spots were exploited in spectacular fashion, with Patrick's voice cracking and turning into a pathetic scream multiple times. Oh, they were able to get him to cum -- it was obvious through a series of trial and error that he found Brian's long toes and strident feet the most attractive of the bunch -- but with each new filmed spray of seed, Patrick's resistance went down. He was tickled and horned into absolute and total submission. By the time he finally shot a dry load, with his violet cock pulsing out nothing but air, all the boys essentially collapsed right then and there, each of them falling into a deep multi-hour sleep. They would all wake up with dirty socks placed on their noses and a Post It note full of individual daily instructions. Patrick dared not ever escape again after that.

Sitting around the table during the present day, Mike was finishing his eggs benedict and Patrick couldn't help but think about the new slaves that Mike was acquiring, and what was so special about them.

"Brian," Mike shouted out, "What did we learn of the boys?"

Brian looked up from the two smartphones he was pouring over for hours. "Oh, I got some good pics. This Atlan guy has a nice-lookin' bank account, sir."

"Oh good," Mike said, putting his napkin down. Dan started putting it away when he caught Nathan hanging out in the doorway, looking.

He snapped his fingers and pointed down to his feet dangling from the kitchen chair. Nathan was trained well: he rushed over and fell to the floor, massaging and licking Mike's bare soles as he sat.

"Tell me," Mike started, "did we find any other playthings of note?"

"I think so," said Brian, standing up and bringing over Jon's phone. "How does this one look?"

Mike inspected it: it was some handsome young twentysomething named Alex who had fluffy, jet-black hair and was sporting a nice pair of glasses. His jawlines were well cut.

"Oh yes," said Mike, "I could see having some fun with this one. Think you'd be able to get him over to the new base tonight?"

"Yes," Brian said. "I've gone over him and Jon's chat history enough that I think I could imitate a good conversation. He'll definitely think he's talking to Jon."

"Excellent," Mike said. "Stop," he ordered the toe-hungry Nathan. "Fetch me my clothes," he demanded. Nathan ran off to grab them.

"Oh, and one more thing," started Brian. He gestured over to Mike to take a look see. "This is this guy named Owen: a bit tall, a friend of Jon's on Facebook, gay, and when I ran a facial recognition search through other databases, it appears that he's an erstwhile dungeon master."

Mike examined the images his slavish little tech wiz was able to procure and enjoyed seeing this 6'5" thin friend of Jon's in a leather harness and leather pants in some sort of sex dungeon. Definitely not something for Facebook, but Brian, being Brian, was able to find it.

"Yeah," Mike commanded, "bring him too. See if you can convince him to show up with his leather accessories. There could be some fun to be had."

"Yes Sir," said Brian, happy to have pleased his Master with a new boytreat, even if meant the life of this person he would never know was going to now circle that of Mike's.

"Sir," Dan started in his monotone voice, "when will we get to see the new place, or even the new slaves?"

Nathan brought Mike's black business socks, shoes, and several hangers. Nathan started as he always did by placing socks right onto Mike's masterful feet. "Play your cards right, and it might even be tonight, boy," said Mike.

Nathan continued dressing him as Mike barked out commands. "Patrick," he shouted, "status report."

Patrick went over to a nearby laptop, glancing at info he had already pulled up. "We made $4,652 yesterday, sir, and had three cam shows."

"Good," Mike stated, as Nathan continued buttoning his master up. "Dan, when was the last time you came?"

"Uhh," Dan started thinking, "I think six days ago? Maybe longer."

"And when was the last time you were on camera for our valued customers?"

"Um, I dunno, maybe like ... four months ago?"

"Got it," said Mike. "Patrick and Nathan, I want you to be in chastity cages today. Put Dan in front of the cam for our paying subscribers. Maybe make a foot vid. I dunno. You whores are always thirsty for attention. You can cum as much as you need to today, Dan."

A smile stretched across Dan's face and he immediately proceeded to get down on his knees and start kissing Mike's now-socked feet. Patrick begrudgingly went over to a drawer that had everyone's chastity cages and started putting one on himself.

"Alright boys," Mike started, "I'm off. Keep your phones on. I may have to have you on standby."

Mike slipped on his shoes and made his way out the door. Any thoughts of his harem of slaves disappeared almost the second the door closed, 'cos they were under his command, making him money with their cumshots without him having to lift a finger. For now though, he was particularly interested to see how well Jon and Atlan were doing at getting his new place assembled -- and just how horny his new slaveboys were.

CHAPTER V: KING OF THE CASTLE

"Fuck, man," pleaded Jon. "Please let me fucking cum!!"

"Not quite yet," said Atlan, who was sitting on a high bar chair that Mike had moved into the apartment. Atlan's legs were dangling off of the chair, but there was Jon, on his knees and bent back a little bit, thrusting his pelvis in the air, his hardon visible an in view of every wall of the apartment. As he knelt in this stress position, Atlan's toes were dangling and circling Jon's nipples, causing Jon's hardon to only pulse in pleasure. Atlan had given him the order to pull away only when he felt like he was about to cum. This has happened about four times so far.

Jon's mind was somewhat shut down. After being teased and sexually tormented like this for ... however long he had been, he was losing track of time. Of thoughts. Of sense of self. Had this been going on for two jam-packed days? Or was it a week? Or was it a year? He was so on the verge of horniness that his IQ had lost a point with each new pulse of his cock, which was basically a foreign agent at this point, operating independently of Jon's thoughts and desires. Well, the cock is his desires. Wait, "is his desires"? The hell kind of thought is that? Jon was second-guessing and questioning every single aspect of his life right now, and while electricity shot through his nipples due to Atlan's torment, all he could do was glimpse at his friend-turned-dom's bare feet now, eyeing each and every ridge of those toe prints and thinking about how badly he wanted to lick them, to kiss them, to suck them. For now though, they were driving him batshit insane.

"Dude, please," Jon pleaded, almost near tears. "Let me cum or let me go."

"I dunno," smirked Atlan, clearly enjoying himself. "It's kind of fun to see you suffer like this. You should be more respectful to Mike. He gave you volumes of pleasure." Atlan's big toes were still circling those fine, hard nips of Jon's.

"Dude, please," Jon said, hard and starting to cry. "I need to cum. Let me cum. Let me cum!!"

"Oh, Jonny boy," started Atlan. "We just moved a bunch of things into a bunch of rooms -- I'm still cooling down. And this is fun. Plus, to see you, naked, kneeling and leaning back with your hips thrusting out -- this stress position is making your fine body glisten with sweat. I'm enjoying the view. Quite a bit, even."

"OK!" Jon screamed. "I'm close to cumming!!"

"You sure?" asked Atlan, teasingly.

"YES!" screamed Jon.

With that, Atlan removed his toes and commanded his Jonslave to relax. Jon collapsed on the hardwood floor, his body exhausted. Jon's manly sweat was so voluminous that it lightly covered the area of the floor he laid on, creating a bit of a mirror for Atlan to view his slave in.

Atlan, although under Mike's commands, wasn't a monster. He walked over to the kitchen and got yet another glass of water for his slave. He brought it over to the heaving Jon and forcibly opened his hand to put the glass of water in (Jon was clearly very weak at this point). After a moment, Jon went and pulled the glass up to take a sip, and drank practically the whole thing all at once.

As he laid there, a knock landed on the door. Atlan glanced at his mostly unconscious friend and said "OK, you wait there. Something tells me that our Master is home." Jon heard this and was wondering if Atlan was even conscious of the fact that the word "Master" was slipping into his sentences.

Atlan, proud, naked, and hard, went to the door and opened it only to see two of Jon's friends standing there: Alex and Owen. Alex was thin and someone who dressed in dark and dry colors, thin as a rail and with flowing, raven-black hair. Owen was the tall goof who had a backpack filled with BDSM leather equipment. They were expecting to see Jon. Brian had chatted to them as if he was Jon via that phone he handed over earlier, and both these friends arrived at about the same time. Upon the door opening, there was a naked and hard Atlan, a friend they had hung out with a few times, but now, well, everything was literally hanging out.

"Oh," said Owen, intrigued. "Um, hi Atlan. How, uh, are you?"

Atlan didn't even feel a remote amount of embarrassment. He felt pride standing there, humiliated, naked as his Master commanded him, showing off his new self to some friends.

"Well hello, gentlemen," declared Atlan. "How are you this fine evening?"

Alex was particularly shaken by what he was seeing. "Um, maybe we caught you at a bad time? Where's Jon? Also, do you, uh, happen to have a towel or shorts or something by chance?"

"Oh, Jonny boy?" smirked Atlan, "He's just getting his rest over there." He pointed to where Jon was laying in a puddle of sweat. Owen and Alex immediately moved past Atlan to go near him.

"My goodness!" declared Alex. "Is he OK?"

"Is he injured?" asked Owen.

"Oh no," said Atlan, still weirdly confident and hard. "He's just exhausted. We've been having our share of erotic games. I've been winning, clearly."

Alex and Owen both looked at Atlan with arched eyebrows.

"I didn't think you were gay," said Alex.

"And I definitely know that Jon isn't," said Owen.

"Yeah, but that dick of his hasn't cum for days, and I've been tasked with keeping him that way. That's why he's so exhausted," Atlan explained.

"Dude, seriously, put some pants on or something!" exclaimed Alex.

"Jon, are you OK?" asked Owen.

Jon was still trying to push through his exhaustion. He was able to make out that his friends were here. He could hear their voices. He looked up at Owen. He looked down at his penis and was amazed to find it still astonishingly hard, desperate to cum even after not being touched for minutes upon minutes.

"Owen," he eked out. "What are you doing here?"

"Better question: why are both you naked?" remarked Alex.

Jon's eyes went wide. "Guys, you have to leave right fucking now. I'm not kidding. This is an emergency. You can't be here when he returns!"

"Who?" asked Owen.

"Me," said Mike, standing in the doorway. "Well, it looks like all of my little chickadees have made it home to roost."

"Hello, Sir!" shouted out Atlan, a big stupid grin on his face as he proved to be surprisingly happy to see his owner return. "Jon's fine, but he's exhausted." Jon managed to get himself into a sitting position by this point.

"Atlan, what the hell is going on?" asked Alex.

"Maybe I can explain," started Mike, walking over to the couch in the living room of the newly, freshly-arranged apartment. "Your friends are having a new experience. Something truly life-changing. They're awakened. Sexually. They suddenly want things that they never thought they'd wanted before, and are free because of it. Here, let me show you: Atlan."

"Yes, Sir?" Atlan stated, perked up like a puppy dog.

"What do you want to do right now? Be honest," Mike stated.

"I'd ... like to take off your shoes and worship your toes, Sir," Atlan said.

"Good," said Michael, placing his feet on the coffee table in front of the couch. "Do that."

Atlan made his way over as Alex and Owen were gathered around Jon. Jon was still propped up, drained, but grabbed both of his friends by the arms. "Guys, please, run. You don't understand. You can't succumb too."

"Dude, what are you talking about?" asked Alex. Atlan started unlacing Mike's shoes during all of this.

"Yeah, this is all kind of freaking me out a bit," admitted Owen.

"Leave me, it's too late for me," gasped Jon.

"It's off," said Mike from the couch, clearly overhearing all of the boys' conversations.

"Fuck," sighed Jon, defeated.

"What?" said Alex. "Whatever freaky sex thing you have going on here has no effect on us."

"Alex," Mike commanded, "stand up and take your shirt off."

Without hesitation, Alex did so, standing upright and removing his shirt to reveal a nice set of abs across his slender frame and pale white skin. The paleness helped highlight just how utterly dark his hair was by contrast. The men in the room all gazed.

"Alex, tell me you're a good little boy," said Mike. Atlan was fixing to untie Mike's other shoe while he continued speaking.

"I'm a good little boy," said Alex, a bit of perplexion in his voice as he was utterly unsure why he was saying what he was being told.

"Owen, come stand next to him," ordered Mike. Owen did so. "Owen, you're gay, right?"

"Yes Sir," responded Owen. Again, Jon noted just how quickly those dominant terms slipped into the speech without Mike even asking.

"Take a look at Alex," Mike continued, both shoes off and his socked feet fumes filling up the room. "Have you ever had fantasies involving him? Things you'd want to do to him?"

"I mean, not really ..." admitted Owen.

"Oh? Well looking at him now, tell me what you'd like him to do to you -- or you to him -- if you fancy him in any way."

"Well," started Owen, his hungry eyes looking up and down the waifish boy's body with allure, "if I had it my way, he seems like he'd be someone that'd be fun to force to suck my cock."

"Does this idea excite you, Owen?" mused Mike.

"Yeah ... it really does," Owen admitted.

"Whip your dick out and start pumping it," ordered Mike.

Owen's pants quickly unfastened and unzipped, revealing a monster 8" dick that was expanding in size with every passing second. Here he was, tall and fully clothed, hardon out and in hand, pumping it right in front of this shirtless straight boy in front of him.

"Alex," asked Mike. "How do you feel?"

"Fucking awkward and upset," admitted Alex. "I don't know what's going on."

"Oh?" asked Mike. "You've never wanted to suck a man's penis before?"

"Goodness no," Alex said with a hint of disgust in his voice.

"Well," started Mike, "what if I told you that deep in your heart of hearts, you've always wanted to suck a man's dick? That you've been craving it, fantasizing about it, but denying that truth to yourself? Tucking it away. You really secretly have wanted to know what it's like, don't you? To be serving a man? To submit your entire being to his whims and desires? To disassociate yourself and all you give into the world in favor of being just a fuckhole for a horned up guy to not off in? How good would that feel, Alex? To be used. To be thrown aside the second that you're done. To have all those intellectual thoughts and concepts you have circling your head be thrown to the wayside just so you can be a bitch just for once. You'd like that, won't you?"

"Yes," said Alex, a sigh of lust in his voice. "I think I'd like that very much."

"Take a look at Owen's cock in front of you. Doesn't it look appetizing?"

"Yes," admitted Alex. "I like it very much."

Mike scoffed. "Very much," he repeated back. "That's funny. Owen, would you like this wisp of a man to put his mouth around your meat python?"

"Actually," said Owen, "I'd like to see him beg for it."

A light went off for Mike. That's right: this guy was in some BDSM dungeons before. His trainings -- and his real desires -- were pressing into the fore. Maybe he wouldn't have to be as "guiding" with this one. Maybe this one could operate independently (outside of a few ground rules, of course).

"You're right," started Mike. "Alex, you want that cock so badly. Take off the rest of your clothes. Start touching yourself. Get hard. Think about how badly you want to wrap your lips around that meat, but know that you can't do anything unless Owen gives you the go-ahead."

Alex unfastened his belt and brought his pants down with intense speed, removing his boxers and socks as the pants went down, soon standing naked and increasingly-hard in front of the small gathering of men. Jon couldn't help but look and gawk but still had next to no strength in his body. Alex got on his knees of the hardwood of the apartment and started stroking himself while staring at Owen's massive member coming out of those unzipped pants. Owen was clearly enjoying the sight of this as time went on.

"Please," said Alex, stroking himself while licking his lips, "I want to suck your cock. Please let me suck your dick, Owen."

Owen started stroking himself. "This dick right here, boy?" he started.

"Yes," said Alex. "I want it. I want it more than anything in the world."

"What would you do to get it, boy?" teased Owen.

"Anything you want, Sir." There was a hint of true desperation in Alex's voice. "Anything at all."

"Be specific," Owen commanded.

Alex, still stroking himself on his knees, was gradually overcome with more and more lust. "I'd ... I'd fucking suck your balls, Sir. I'd lick the tops of your feet and suck on your toes. I'd let you stick your sweaty socks in my mouth and then proceed to tape it in while you torture my body with whatever hot thing you want to do. Fuck. I'd stick my tongue down your ass if you want it, Sir. I'd let you put me in chastity while you also put a vibrating butt plug up my ass and leave it in there to see how long it takes me to go insane."

"Keep going," smirked Owen, enjoying the spectacle.

"I'll be your fuckin' sex toy!" screamed Alex, so delirious with horniness that he was practically in tears. "What do you want? I'll let you tie me up! I'll let you tickle me until I go insane! I'll let you edge me and film it while pegging me or just flat-out fucking me. Please! I just want to suck your cock!"

Mike smirked. He nodded his head.

"Houston, we're clear for takeoff," started Owen. "Go ahead, boy. Start with just the head."

Jon felt a wave of exhaustion take over him like he had never felt before. The day had taken a physical and emotional toll on him. He eyesight grew bleary and out of focus. He saw the shape of a kneeling Alex lean in to Owen's crotch, accepting the meat and the pre at the tip of it, but that's all Jon saw. It was the last thing he could remember seeing, at least, before he passed out then and there.

CHAPTER VI: FEET DREAMS

Jon woke up on ... was this hay?

There was a coldness to the air around him. His head was groggy. His last memory was simple: Alex was on his knees about to service Owen. He thought. Or was it all a dream? It was hard to say.

All Jon knew is that he was confused, frustrated, and horrendously unsatisfied. Here he was: a nice guy living in the big city looking for a roommate so that way his rent wasn't absolutely insane. It seemed like a simple enough request. He wasn't expecting to go on some dude's fucked up journey of sexual pleasure, forced on him unwillingly. Now he was doing stuff with dudes -- but not even dudes, his actual real-life friends. It's like a hand was grabbing the back of his head and forcing it down onto his friends' bare toes, kept down there long enough that he was starting to like it. There is no way to describe what it feels like to have someone else's weird little fetish shoved inside your brain, much less one that shows no signs of going away anytime soon.

Yet the worst part about all of this was that Jon was fighting a part of himself. He thought about all his awkward bedroom fumblings with girls in high school and college, the one-night stands and awkward condom adjustments he had to make. He always enjoyed sex (who didn't) but never felt the pangs of true love. He was a bit of a romantic drifter, moving from fuck to fuck with little luck. While he always wanted more from his sex and romantic life, he had somewhat resigned himself to a fate of being mostly single for as far as the future could hold him.

What Mike had shown him, however, was pure passion. Not just full-tilt lust (which this very much was), but genuine and unflinching passion. Of loving something so much that your entire body, mind, and soul aches for it. That kind of passion. Getting lost in it. Finding pathways in it. He had gone through every stage of lust imaginable and he was certain more than a few stages that mankind had never considered before too. As much as he hated being thrust into a sexual nightmare, there was something refreshing about feeling about something in a way that ignites his bones (and boner), that makes him think almost outside of himself, that achieves a primal kind of reaction which is beyond that almost bordered on a religious experience.

But none of these revelations left Jon in a state of gratitude. He was more upset that all of this forced upon him suddenly. Much as how he was forced into this weird room, which was -- wait, where the hell was he?

There was a weird weight that took him a few seconds to identify. Yes, it was on his neck: a giant metal collar. Jon was trying to get his bearings: he was sleeping in what appeared to be some sort of ... tower? Like a medieval spire of some sort? There was hay on the floor in the rough shape of a bed, and stone cold walls and floors made of unattractive brown brick. Jon was naked save for his giant metal neck collar and a very small, very simple leather loincloth. There was a bit of fabric hanging out over the front of his junk but anyone staring at it for more than two seconds would still catch sight of his cock or balls.

Jon also noticed that his neck collar was connected to a metal chain, but not one which was dead-bolted to a wall. Instead, it was fed through a hole in a door. Being an apparently medieval tower, the door was made of wood. It was almost cartoonish in design. Yet the hole in the door was actually a rectangle shape that went all the way to the edge of the door, as if the chain were dragged into the room beyond the door and that door were to open, the chain would slip out the side and then ... he'd be in the other room.

Quite literally as Jon thought that the chain did as he predicted, dragging him by the neck slowly towards the door. Jon had no idea where he was or what was going on but figured that unknown forces forcing him to move into new locales was probably not a good thing.

He tried planting his bare feet on the floor and gaining traction but the weight of this pulling thing was so significant that Jon thought it had to be mechanical. He nonetheless grabbed the chain with his arms and tried to pull but to no avail. Throughout all of this, he was rather struck by his own reaction to the whole affair. Here he was, seemingly locked in a tower, and wasn't 1000% panicking by how he even got here. It's as if his mind and body had accepted this scenario as its own thing, which made him wonder: was any of this real? Was he dreaming?

As he got closer to the door, it expectedly flung open, with the chain slipping out the side and pulling him into the next room. Yet whatever was in the next room was filled with light: overwhelming, blinding light. With one hand still trying to hold on to his pulling chain, another one went up over his eyes to protect them from the glare, and then, without warning ...

... wood. He was in stocks. He was standing, still with a loincloth, but his head and hands were all locked in wooden stocks. He could look to the left to see his left hand, to the right to see his right, but those were restrained now: he was standing in some basic-yet-evil stocks. And he was standing ... on stage. The light had faded and Jon, bleary-eyed, could make out some shapes: faces. Older men's faces. Gradually, his ears tuned in to the sound as well. Hoots. Hollers. Cheers and leers. The room was dark, small, seedy. The kind of place where you'd find an illegal cockfight -- the backroom of some restaurant or something.

Yet here Jon was, on a small wooden stage, head and arms in stocks that made him stand fully upright, his junk covered by a loincloth and nothing else. He heard chants and shouts and vulgar phrases -- and then realized that they were all directed at him.

"Isn't he fabulous, boys!" came a shout on stage. Jon glanced over and saw a youngish looking man with a bald head, sturdy black beard, and thin build. He had on pants that were vaguely poofy and an unbuttoned vest going over his otherwise-shirtless torso. No shoes. And he had abs to boot. The man then looked directly at Jon's face.

"Oh my, he doesn't know what's going on, does he?" the man said with some sass in his voice. This lead to some laughter from the crowd.

"Uhh," is all Jon managed to get out, which lead to more laughter from the crowd.

"It's OK, it's OK," said the man on stage. "You're confused, you're disoriented -- I'm gonna set you straight. Well, as straight as we allow here." More guffaws from the crowd. Jon's nostrils detected the smell of cigar smoke. This really was a boozy, sin-filled place.

"My name," the man started, "is Pervy Pat, and I'm here to help all of these other pervs figure out if you're good for sellin'! What do you say, boys? Does he look appetizing or what?" Cheers and applause from the peanut gallery.

"S-selling?" mumbled out Jon, still very confused.

"Yes, boy," said Pat as he dragged Jon by the neck chain to center stage. "You are stock and trade, now. You're some sort of blow boy, someone who's only going to exist for the pleasure of whoever decides to spend thousands upon thousands of dollars to own you. Your mouth is going to get verrrrrrry used, let me tell you." This garnered more crowd laughter. "However, these fine gentlemen in the audience have had their share of male meat and have seen all the ins and outs and ups and downs. These rich and powerful and *beautiful* men own fellas of every time: bodybuilders and frat boys and nerdlingers and cubs and you name it. You, Jon, with your supple and intriguing frame, may fetch a high price, but first we gotta test some things, right?"

The audience cheered at this. Jon was taking this all in and still unsure of what to think, say, or feel. His arms were starting to feel a little tired being held at the same level his head is at by the stocks.

"So first off, Jonny Boy," started Pat, "why don't you lift one of them legs up for me?"

Involuntarily, Jon lifted his leg up, standing on one foot. Pat grabbed the outstretched leg and seemed intent on showing the bottom of Jon's sole to the crowd. Jon was trying to maintain his balance while on one leg and in stocks at the same time. Pervy Pat ran his nose along the hairs of Jon's shins and inhaled all sorts of scent.

"Boys," Pat shouted, "I don't know if you can smell it from here, but goodness this boy's sweat is divine. Mmm, he is a *snack!* Now, you boys out there in the audience, look at these toes and arches. Do you footpervs out there see something you like?"

The response was nothing but hoots and hollers. A few coins were tossed up onto stage. Jon could barely see them with his head immobilized by the wooden stock but somehow, even though he couldn't make out the coins clearly, just knew that they were a different type of currency, and each coin was worth at least $100. Some maybe more. He had zero idea how he knew that.

Pat leaned over and licked the edge of Jon's big toe. For whatever reason, the sensation of that moist muscle made Jon's spine jerk upright. The crowd laughed.

Pervy Pat licked his lips in almost comical fashion while letting Jon's leg settle back to the floor. "Boys, I know I just said it, but let me repeat: this boy is gonna be a tasty addition to whatever dungeon you have in mind." More cheers. More coins being thrown on stage. While everyone may want to be desired in one way or another, Jon definitely didn't want it to be like this, so lasciviously and carnally.

"Ohhhh boys," started Pat again. "I think it's time to see if our boy Jon here is a bit of a curtain peeker, don't you?"

This garnered a roar of approval from the crowd.

Jon was worried. "What in--"

"Quiet," commanded Pat, and just like that, Jon didn't feel like he could say words anymore. Pat moved behind him, putting his torso and legs and loincloth out there on the main stage for all to see. Jon was the star, the main attraction now. And then slowly, he felt Pat's arms go around either side of him and -- no, no fucking way.

Pat's fingertips started lightly circling and playing with Jon's nipples, which, due to the physical touch they were receiving, were only getting harder by the minute. The feeling was agonizing: with little rotations, Jon's nipples felt every ridge of those fingerprints move along his sensitive pecs, each swipe and flick sending just a bit more electricity down his body and into his groin. One more flick, one more gathering of sensation down there. Although he was virtually nothing but terrified by everything that was going on, Pervy Pat was converting that terror into a turnon with each and every flick.

Then Jon realized what he meant by being a "curtain peeker": the scrap of leather that was the front of his loincloth was so small, that as soon as he started getting hard, that boner of his inflated and humiliatingly start peaking through the cfloth, at first gradually and then eventually putting the entire cloth over to one side, his hardon now out there in full force in front of the entire room.

The worst part of all of this is how even though Pervy Pat's nipple teasings were getting him all worked up and almost forgetful how horrifying his situation was, there was a part of Jon that ... was enjoying being humiliated? Of having his cock teased out from a piece of clothing in front of everyone to see? Of having his nipples -- a true blue turnon for him -- being exploited so powerfully and significantly? Being a lust object for men who lust so openly and brazenly?

"Winner winner chicken dinner!" Pat declared. "Oh yes, for modest sums of your entire fortune, you can have this easily-teaseable, ready-to-pleaseable piece of manflesh at your beck and call. Can I get an Amen up in here?"

A boozy chorus rang out an "Amen" all its own, like some sort of sick church service that worshiped lust and seed above all else. Pervy Pat was eating it all up, but soon had ideas all his own.

"OK, Jonathan," Pat sneered, "I think we should give the boys what they really came out to see, don't you?"

Jon tried to make some response but still couldn't after Pervy Pat's last command.

"Oh, silly me, you still can't speak," he declared. "... let's keep it that way. Now turn and face me."

Jon, still at the front of the stage, turned and faced Pervy Pat, Jon's arms still near his head in the wooden stocks.

"Now get down on your knees," Pat ordered. As Jon did so, a sitcom-level "Ooooh," came from the audience, goading Pat on.

"In your current state of ... binding," Pat started, "you can't necessarily get a good view of what I think you really, secretly, in your heart of hearts want to look at."

A pregnant pause filled the air.

"Bend over," Pat commanded.

Jon did so, letting his arm/head stocks slam on the floor of the stage as he got insanely close to Pat's bare toes, sticking out of those loose entertainer pants he was wearing. He was instantly turned on, suddenly filled with lust, and craved nothing more than putting Pat's toes in his mouth. Of course, as he stuck out his tongue, he realized that with his head on the ground and his legs kneeling -- his but was in the air, meaning his tight pink asshole was in full sight of the entire gallery. Jon heard them all react but wasn't exactly sure what the sound they made was. He was in stocks, so couldn't exactly get a good view behind him: just what was in front of him. Pat's toes.

Pervy Pat saw the boy starting to geek out on those thick toes and perfectly-shaped and trimmed toenails in front of him, and decided to pull up the rim of his loose pants a bit so that the tops of his feet were visible. Right on the tops of both his feet were tattoos. Words. "You're A" read one foot, "Foot Slave" read the other.

"Now," Pat stage-whispered to Jon, "while these men put in their bids, why don't you give them a show?"

Jon's tongue reached out and Pat moved his masculine toes closer. Jon estimated they were about a size 10.5 from what he could see.

His tongue licked the top of one toe and -- he felt something! What was that? It was like a feather ran up his asshole real quick. Well, not a feather, but ... was that a tongue?

Pat snapped his fingers. "Pay attention to what's important, slave," he said. "Get back to it."

Seeing the tattoos on both tops, he decided to do what felt right and drag his tongue across the words "Foot Slave", and as he did so, felt a tongue lick his asshole at the same speed. He shuddered ... but it also felt so good. He had to be in a dream, right? Dream logic would support some insane fantasy like this, where the more his own tongue gets to touch his objects of desire, the more someone else's tongue(s) get to match the intensity in his asshole.

"Keep doing it, puppy," Pat commanded, and just like with Mike's commands, Jon plowed through, licking and slobbering over Pat's tops and toes while a mysterious set of tongues did the same to his soft, sensitive asshole. He kept licking and therefore kept feeling sensual anal stimuli, those moist, eager tongues getting right in his asshole and touching on all his pleasure centers, which now only made him want to lick more like the fuckin' footperv he is and it created a sick cycle and Pat was cheering and the men were laughing and prices were being shouted out and good fuck he just couldn't take it anymore HOLY SHIT JON WAS GONNA CUM HIS COCK WAS BEET RED AND GOING TO EXPLODE RIGHT THEN AND THERE!--

And then everything changed.

He ... heard a cart move by? Curtains. White curtains. Where was he? He could move his hands. Yet, he couldn't. No, he could, but where was he? Carpet. His chin felt carpet. His chin? That was weird. Jon closed his eyes for a second and reopened them to get his bearings. Where was he? Table legs, hints of chairs. He was ... under the table of a restaurant. Someplace fancy. French maybe. The white tablecloth draped things pretty nicely but Jon could almost see through them and heard dessert carts being moved by, the occasional clanging of silverware, some out-of-focus conversations. General restaurant ambiance.

Yet, what was he doing? His head was under the center of this table. Just his head. The rest of his body was somehow underneath the floor of the restaurant, but Jon couldn't exactly pinpoint what it was doing. If he was just "hanging by his neck" under the restaurant floor, he'd be in pain, but he wasn't. He wasn't submerged in liquid or anything else. His body was just ... there. Secondary. All that seemed to matter was the fact that his head was poking out of the floor of this restaurant, directly under a circular dinner table. Jon tried turning to the left and right and could do so with smoothness and ease. What -- what was going on?

After a few minutes had passed, he heard the waiter bring over a group of guys over to his table and pull up the chairs. Jon looked around and saw about, yes, four different guys. He didn't see their faces, but just their pants and shoes. There was some business-type with dark blue business pants, slip-on dress shoes and what appeared to be sheer socks. There was some preppy country club type in shorts and boat shoes (and oh my: look at the hair on his legs). There was some fratboy type also in shorts, but wearing actual flip-flops with some nice, beefy toes that clearly belonged to an athlete. Also, there was a light dusting of hair on the top of those toes. Then, there was some regular dad type in blue jeans and with New Balance sneakers on, wahite socks under that. It seemed like a random amalgam of people, but Jon had to remember this was all utterly surreal, so it didn't have to make sense. Mostly.

As he heard commotions of rattling silverware and muted dinner-speak, Jon swerved his head around to get a glimpse of all the feet around him. It was all he could see and all he wanted to focus on. He was still, even after all he had been through and all he had sen, craving feet. That fetish that Mike had implanted in him absolutely has taken hold, and now he was shameless about how much he saw toes and soles as the perfect masculine form, begging to be submitted to and worshiped. Feet were his fucking world now, and while the concept was something he had been fighting out this whole time, maybe his brain was finally breaking and accepting the fact that he was a goddamn foot addict. Or maybe this is just how he was thinking in the logic of a dream.

So for obvious reasons, he turned and looked at the nice, slightly hair toes sitting in the flip-flops, the frat boy's movements and thoughts interpreted through toe wiggles. There was twitching, scrunching -- all very small, subconscious actions. Maybe if they were studied long enough, a kind of sign language could be developed, and seeing a man's toe movements is all you needed to read his mind and his innermost thoughts. Jon felt hypnotized. He couldn't stop watching those toes fidget and move. While he was unsure exactly what the state of his body was below his neck, the one thing he was sure of is that he was fucking horny and lusty, and his mind was soon dominated by the thought that the only thing he wanted in his mouth was those toes.

Then he heard the sound of a shoe slipping off skin, and turned to the side to see the preppy dude's legs with the boat shoes casually slip them off. The second they did, Jon could feel that smell wafting towards his nose, and it did nothing but absolutely excite him. Instead were some beefy size 12s with a wide toebase, those plump pink toes looking like mealworms just begging for a sucking. Suddenly, that too was what Jon wanted, that smell stinging his nose in the best of ways and working its way into the folds of his brain. Yes, please, give me the goddamn feet. Please. The feet. The feet.

Behind him, there was more rustling. He swerved his head around to see a pair of dad arms reach down and start undoing the white laces of those New Balance sneakers. The second they were loose enough, the shoes slipped off. The businessman sitting next to him easily slipped off his work shoes, revealing the hints and shadows of long, masculine toes poking through what was clearly now sheer fabric. Jon was intrigued. He liked the very sight of those toes in those sheers, the way the sock accentuated the shape of those toes and the big foot overall. It's something Jon wanted now. He wanted to be teased, to be tormented with his addiction using hints and tricks like the way these sheer socks were utterly beguiling to him.

Oh, but then those white dad socks. That little bit of dust and sweat forming a pattern on the soles, where there was a hint of smell but primarily just a vague outline of the fat size 10s contained within. Oh, to massage them. Oh, to sniff them, or -- even better -- to sneak in sniff when he's not looking while you're massaging them. Doesn't that sound like bliss? Like paradise?

Seemingly at the very thought of this desire, the two socked men began grabbing the rim of their foot garments and pulling them down, slowly and surely, ensuring that there were now four pairs of bare male feet under the table that Jon's horny head was at. His eyes went wide and a dumb horny smile immediately grabbed his face, so giddy with the thrill of his fantasy coming through. There was only one problem though: by being directly under the center of the table, his head was unable to reach those toes even if he wanted to. It was an island of temptation and he was all alone there, which, in turn, just made him all the harder.

Then, as if wish fulfillment was the name of the game, the entire table above him seemed to shrink in a bit, and as such, the men around him drew in closer. The table didn't disappear, but it was smaller, up to the point where all these feet were now ... inches from Jon's face. All these toes laying flat on the carpet of the restaurant, surrounding him. Jon's head swerved around, looking at all of them, admiring all the little details of each: the roundness and but of the toenails, the size of the big toes, the distinct smells and flavors of each. He loved them all for different reasons. He could stick out his tongue but he still couldn't reach them -- that he knew. And then, the frat boy's feet lifted up and Jon saw long, slender, youthful soles staring back at him. In a second, they carefully pressed onto his face, overwhelming him with flavor and submission.

Jon was elated, happy, stoned off of how hot this was. As he did that, the dad's feet went and pressed up on the back of his head, holding it in place so he couldn't wiggle out of his forced fratboy footmask. Then the businessman and the preppy type placed their toes right on his head and started wiggling them, toes tapping along his skull, each one a soft reminder of what a foot addict he was. This was fucking foot overload right now. Jon couldn't even fucking believe it. All that was in his skull was feet and now all that was surrounding his head was gorgeous, masculine male feet. On all sides. In all ways. All the fucking feet.

"Lick," the dad said, and Jon started lapping at the soles of the fratboy. "Lick," said the businessman, his voice lower but forceful. "Lick," said the preppy kid, a sneer in his voice. "Lick," said the fratboy, almost as a dare to Jon. Jon started lapping but the toes on his head kept tapping and the fratboy left his feet there for worship but the dad used his bare soles to press Jon's head further and further into worship and goodness it was all too much. Jon was a fucking footpig. As soon as he had that thought, that's what all the men started chanting. "Foot-pig! Foot-pig! Foot-pig!" It was growing in volume, unmissable to any other patron of this restaurant, but it's all Jon wanted: he wanted to have his very nature pointed out to him. How humiliating and how fucking horny. Yeah, he was a goddamn footpig, and he was proud of it. He wanted more of it. Licking and smell and toe-tapping and then the chanting and -- fuck -- he was gonna cum. FUCK YEAH HE WAS GONNA CUM! HE WAS GOING TO CUM 'COS HE LOVES BARE MALE FE--

CHAPTER VII: THE REVELATION

"Fuck!" Jon shouted as he shot up, bolt-like.

He was in a dead sweat. The room he was in was dark. He was ... in ... his new room. In bed. Yes, the new room. His old room was what Mike wanted, so he and Atlan set it up. He set up this new room and ... yeah. It was night. He was in sheets. He was fucking horny. He wanted feet. But more on ... what just happened?

Oh yes, that dream. He just woke up from a fuckin' horndog of a dream, didn't he? He looked down on his cock, hard and of a deep purple color, and realized he hadn't cum in days. He had been goaded into cumming, teased beyond all possible existence, but here he was, in his room, unafraid. He grabbed his aching meatrod and starting jacking it ever so lightly -- it felt so good. It felt so fucking good. That's when it struck Jon: he was in a new room. He was unattended. The door was closed. There was a light coming in from under it and he definitely heard sounds coming through the wall: yelps and laughter and moans. Yes, the boys were very much under Mike's command and living out his dreams and fantasies. Jon knew what he would be walking into.

Yet there was a window in his room. His mind was racing from one idea to the next, and yes, even though this was a second-floor walk-up, he could climb out the window and drop down to the ground, fleeing this sexual hell he was trapped in. He could bring cops over but ... no, they too would fall under his spell too, wouldn't they?

But wait: he could touch his cock. He could jack it. Did Mike even plant a command forbidding him to jerk off? Maybe he did, but if it was long enough ago -- maybe it wore off. Maybe he could cum right now. Oh goodness, *he could cum right now if he wanted too!*

Then, it struck him.

The setup. The buildup. The teasing. The tormenting. Sure, maybe Jon hadn't fully realized every part of his sexuality -- maybe there were some kinks left unexplored. The more Jon thought about the male foot fetish in his head now, the more he realized it was now going to be there forever. It took hold so quickly and so strongly that

Jon had to admit it was a part of him now. So why fight it, if that's the case? Maybe he should embrace it. In fact, if he came on his own volition to the thoughts of male feet then ...

That was it. It all made sense. Mike was cruel, no doubt, but also exacting. He saw something in Jon, and he made full use of it. This, right now, was the final test. Cut off from the world, free of commands, Jon was free to make a choice. He could touch that raging erection right now and have the orgasm of his life -- or he could push himself even further. He could go beyond mere orgasmic pleasure. And that's what Mike wanted. Mike knew what he was doing. So it was time to confront him.

Jon stepped out of the bed, himself still fully naked, and walked to the door. He was mid-range hard right now. He opened the door and couldn't believe what he saw.

There was Atlan, on his back on the couch, holding his legs in the air. Kneeling before him was Owen in a leather harness and leather pants, but with his monster cock out, stiff and ready. It wasn't inside of Atlan's ass, but it was circling it, teasing it. Owen was making Atlan beg for it and beg for it hard.

"You want my cock, boy?" Owen teased.

"Yes Sir," said Atlan, tears streaming down his face, "I want your cock so badly, daddy." Jon knew exactly what was going on: Owen or Mike put some sort of command in him where he craved to be fucked in the ass more than anything else in this world, and Owen had been teasing him with his massive member for some untold amount of time, probably sticking just the tip in to get his juices flowing but then pulling out and watching him scream and beg. Jon recognized that sense of desperation on Atlan: he wanted that dick more than anything he's ever wanted anything right now. That lust was pulsating through his body.

Jon glanced past those two and saw Michael, still in a business getup with bare feet sticking out of dress pants, tormenting Alex. Michael was sitting in a reclining leather chair with extendable leg support, his feet extending off of the propped-out legrest. Making them about a foot and a half suspended in the air. Standing next to them was a nude Alex, his cock inserted into a hard plastic black chastity device -- so dark it almost matched his hair. He was standing, staring at Mike's toes, hands behind his back, and making some sort of grimacing face. Was he in pain? No, Jon noticed: he was in questionable sexual agony. He saw that Mike had some sort of remote control in his hand, and then deduced the obvious, devious truth: Alex had a remote-controlled, vibrating buttplug stuck inside him. Now no doubt awash with foothorny desires, Mike was making him suffer by locking him up and making him stare at his objects of lust while his ass succumbs to a dull hum of pleasure.

"Do you like what you see?" asked Mike, matter of factually, wiggling his gigantic toes to Alex's hungry, lust-craved eyes.

"Yes," moaned out Alex, his boner filling up every inch of his manufactured cock cage, unable to get hard as his the remote-controlled playtoy teased his virgin prostate. He was trying to hold back tears he was so horny -- just like Atlan. Mike was really doing a number on these boys.

Yet Jon wasn't here to save them, despite his better instincts. He was here to end this erotic charade once and for all.

"Hey!" he shouted, and all four men looked directly at Jon, stopping their motions. It would've been pindrop silent were it not for the hum of Alex's vibrating butt plug.

"It's time," Jon shouted, wielding an otherworldly level of confidence.

"... for ... what?" asked Master Mike.

Jon didn't even respond. He walked over to Mike's laid-back recliner and mounted it, his bent legs over Mike's thighs, leaned in, and kissed Mike directly on the mouth. Jon's tongue went in, and Mike's own tongue was cautious at first before giving in. He was surprised but welcoming to Jon's sudden affections.

They pulled their lips away from each other and stared. Jon's erection was again at full tilt.

"You realize," Jon said, "that after this is over, you will be punished."

Mike smiled. "You can do whatever you like after -- I just want it to work."

"It has to be the feet, right?" asked Jon.

"Yes," said Mike,' "but embellish however you wish."

"Give me control over them," Jon asked. The boys all looked over at the two talking men, unsure of what the hell they were on about. It's like some sort of mental conversation happened that filled in all the details but they were unsure of what it all meant.

Mike hesitated for a moment -- something entirely not in his observed nature so far -- but granted Jon's wish.

"Boys," Mike commanded, "do whatever Jon wants." They all were now standing at casual attention, ready to receive orders. Jon dismounted from Mike's recliner and faced them. Mike switched Alex's vibrating butt plug off. Alex sighed in relief.

"Alex," Jon said with a sense of true command, "go to the kitchen, remove that butt plug and wash it thoroughly. It's about to go in me."

Alex nodded and walked off to the kitchen.

"Owen and Atlan," Jon started, "get feathers and vibrating cock rings. Get ready, 'cos this could happen at any moment."

Both boys looked at Mike. "My room, under the bed, black cabinet, top drawer," Mike informed them. They both hustled off.

With just Mike and Jon in the room, there was an excitement in the air.

"This might be your last moment to be in this position," Jon said, touching and tugging himself on and off.

"I don't think you understand," Mike said, "I've been working for years for this."

"So why me?" asked Jon. "If this is going to happen, then how did you know?"

"Trial and error," Mike said. "You could even call this fate, but the second I had you under my control, I could feel something was different. You had it in you."

There was a pause.

"So ... what's going to happen?" said Jon.

"Well," Mike said, "it's kind of win-win for you, as you're either going to have the best orgasm of your life -- perhaps even the best known to mankind -- or you're going to ... see more than the sliver that I saw."

Jon smiled at this. "Well, I can't complain."

"Just ... please be merciful if you turn," asked Mike, showing a sign of vulnerability for perhaps the first time ever.

Jon simply looked back at him and gave a simple answer: "No."

Alex, Atlan, and Owen returned, tools all in hand. Jon was still hard. Actually, they all were, but Jon's dick, which astoundingly hadn't cum after days of erotic torment, was thicker, redder, and more magnetic than the others' by a large margin. They guys were all staring at it.

"OK fellas," started Jon, "the name of the game is going to be pleasing me. Pleasing me like I've never been pleased before. You're all going to help me achieve orgasm. Mike is going use his perfect, gorgeous feet and plant them on my face. He'll also control the butt plug. Atlan and Owen, you'll be licking my nipples. Alex, you'll be dragging that feather along my shaft after the vibrating cockring is placed over the head. You got it?"

"Yes," they all agreed.

"I'll be on the floor," stated Jon. "Let's get ready. "

Over the next few minutes, Jon was prepared and pampered like some sort of sexy astronaut about to go on a mission. He bent over and Alex carefully inserted the butt plug, taking a few tries before it got in and tight, pressed right up against Jon's prostate. The vibrating cock ring was placed around Jon's cockhead, right under the lip of that pink helmet, but not turned on yet. Mike took the chair he was sitting on out of reclining position so his feet were flush with the floor. Jon laid down, laying his head on the top of Mike's masculine bare feet while the boys surrounded him.

"You ready?" asked Mike.

"Let's do this," started Jon.

"Good. Now stare at it, slave," started Mike, lifting his feet up now and placing them right above Jon's face, filling up his field of vision with nothing but glorious male bare soles. Alex pressed a button on the cockring and it started pulsating slowly, sending waves of pleasure through Jon's thick member. Fuck, he was close to cumming already. Then, perched on the floor, Owen and Atlan leaned in from the sides and started romantically licking and flicking Jon's nipples with their tongues.

"Fuck," Jon said, and he knew there was no going back now. The licking of his nips was so intense that it made his dick twitch, which in turn made the vibrating cock ring feel all the more intense. Around this time, Alex then started taking soft, firm-edged feathers to Jon's veiny, beet-red shaft, slowly dragging it along that flesh, each stroke feeling like sexual lightning coursing through his body.

At that point, Mike flicked the button on a remote, causing the vibrations to start in Jon's prostate which made him almost pop up from the ground but instead his face just went right into Mike's feet, which proceed to slowly press Jon's face down into the floor and keep it there.

"You have a foot fetish, Jon," commanded Mike, "and you fucking love it. You want to cum over how much you love the feeling of my bare male feet on your face right now."

At that moment, all Jon could feel was Mike's beautiful masculine feet on him. Mike turned the remote control all the way up as Jon, who was just drooling precum right now, felt that and his nipples being licked and his cock being stroked and vibrated all at. His balls churned with pent-up energy, and he realized he was at the point of no return. His body was reacting in a huge way it never had before, pleasure coming in from every possible angle and in every possible form. Although Mike's feet cover his face, all he could do was just scream into those toes in a guttural, primal way that was beyond what any human had ever experienced before. It all ended with one word, shouted with more fury and joy and anguish than any human ever has before in history:

"FUUUUUUUUUUUUUUCCCCCCCCCCCCCCCCCCKKKKKKK KKKKKKKK!!!"

...

Jon was tranquil. He was naked. He was still hard. All around him was just white. White space. He could breathe, he could jump (if he wanted to), and all his senses were working. But instead, he was just in this space. This empty space. Didn't he just cum? Where was he?

Time seemed to be passing, but, also -- not. It was hard to define. Jon tried tugging at his insane erection but no matter what he seemed to do, his amount of pleasure fluctuated in only the smallest of amounts. Its as if it was "locked" in place or stuck or something. Jon was profoundly confused by what was going on.

"Hey man!" a voice said behind him. It was unfamiliar to Jon. He turned around. "How's it going?"

Here stood a man in bare feet, blue jeans, and a plain white shirt, so clean it almost bled into the white background of whatever space the two were occupying right now. He was a hair under six feet tall and had a roundish face: well built but with curling brown hair and a beard that somewhat circled his face. It was a bit unkempt.

"Don't be scared," the guy said, "it's all pretty weird, I know, but you're in good company. I'm Gage!"

He extended his hand. Jon, nude and with a too-obvious erection, questionably shook the hand in return.

"I'm ... Jon?" Jon said, unsure of what to do here.

"You're good, man," Gage said. "I think you've earned a bit of a break, haven't you?"

"From what?" asked Jon. Gage got a puzzled look on his face.

"Um, from everything that Mike put you through? Ensnaring your friends into becoming fuckable sex slaves while forcing fetishes into your brain and making you not cum for days on end with virtually no sleep? That ring a bell?"

"I mean, yeah," said Jon, sheepishly. Gage laughed.

"Oh man, you're taking this all so *seriously!* Trust me dude, you're good," Gage said.

"So where are we?" Jon said. Gage started walking side-by-side with Jon, even though, in this void, there was seemingly nowhere to walk to.

"I can't really say," Gage explained, "but know that you are on a plane that's different from what most humans experience. It's a plane of pleasure, really."

"Pleasure?" said Jon. "Then why can't I nut?"

Gage guffawed at this. "Oh man! Don't worry. I'm here to experience your last moments of sexual dissatisfaction. After this, you're gonna be good for fuckin' life, dude."

"How so?" Jon inquired.

"Well," Gage started, "you can call me Gage 'cos I'm actually a guy you met during your student film days. I was hoping you'd recognize me but if you don't, that's OK. I wanted to go with something familiar. In fact, this is all a big ol' front. I'm actually just a disciple of Aizen Myō-ō."

"... the fuck?" said Jon.

"It's OK," laughed Gage, "I don't expect you to know who he is, or even how to pronounce it. In short, Aizen is the god of lust, and he converts lust into spiritual awakenings. Listen, the brief rundown is this -- and it's kind of a bummer, but trust me: we are beings given sentience and self-awareness, and we what we do in this life kind of matters. In billions of years, we'll be nothing, but for now, we are to experience the joys and pleasures that have been afforded to us, and let me tell you, Aizen is so fucking frustrated when he sees people milling about and wasting their lives. People go skydiving sometimes and feel a rush of adrenaline but that's only temporary, ya know? Why aren't you experiencing life in all of its joy, all of its feelings, all of its emotions? You can and everyone can and most people just settle for 'good enough.' I think of it as a monster. The monster of Good Enough.

"People sign up for life partners they're only kinda happy with. They settle for sex that's fun but not mind-blowing. They resign themselves to lives of mostly-happiness. It's a cycle. Aizen loves love, mind you, 'cos when you get that first pitter-patter being with someone who cares about you just as much as you care about them? Oh, it's damn close. But man, lust is something else. Not being horned up -- we all know what that feels like -- but when you crave and yearn for something more than just about anything else and you feel like your entire being is building up to this moment? Well, that's what Aizen fuckin' *loves*. He wants people to experience more of that."

"Uh," started Jon, "so like, does he have powers? Can't he just make the whole world become one sort of fuck fest?"

"Heh," smirked Gage, "I wish. That'd be easy. Do you know how few wars people would have if everyone was fuckin' all the time? Oh man, we'd all be so much nicer to each other. But no -- he's not allowed in the realm that you know as reality. I'm not either. However, some people every once in awhile transport over here, albeit temporarily. We can imbue them with powers to take back to the reality that you know, and they can use them to get all sorts of wonderful and naughty and pleasurable things done."

Jon nodded, starting to figure it all out. "So Mike was one of your disciples."

"Yes," said Gage, "he got in a really drunken session with a hookup one night and came while the guy was having him lick his soles. I don't like dealing with people that are intoxicated -- unless they're gettin' high off of horniness, ya know? -- but I still conveyed to him everything I could. I mean, it makes sense he came to me, as I deal with feet and shoes and all sorts of podiacal wonders. I'm in the form of Gage, but to you, you can just call me Footgod."

"Footgod?" said Jon with his eyebrows arched.

"Yeah," said Gage. "You got a problem with that?"

"Uhh, no," started Jon. "I just think it's weird."

"I mean, you have a foot fetish now, right Jon?" asked Gage. Jon's eyes darted to look at Gage's toes but he tried to be discreet.

"I mean, I guess, yeah," he said, a bit sheepish.

"That's funny," Gage said. "And yes, I saw that. It's OK. Look as much as you want."

Jon looked down at Gage's toes and they were so nicely shaped, mid-range long and well-kept. Beautiful and masculine and perfect all at once.

"See?" said Gage, wiggling his toes. "It's nice. It's nice to get hard for these, no?"

"I mean sure," Jon, trying not to give in to temptation. "They're nice."

"Heh," said Gage. "You're trying to fight it. Do you like flip-flops?"

"I mean, they're fine, sure," said Jon.

"OK," said Gage, "how about ... now?"

Gage pressed his thumb to Jon's forehead for a second, and Jon's eyes instantly rolled up to the top of his skull. Gage let his thumb go, and Jon collapsed to the ground.

"What was that?" said Jon, unnerved and starting to jack his dick again.

"That," Gage said, was sending you through five whole years of foot fetish experiences, all involving flip-flops. Do you have any that you remembered? I liked the one of you going up to that tourist in Aruba on the beach who fell asleep under his umbrella on the beach and you took his sandals off with your teeth and jerked off into them right then and there. Oooh, and that Master in Detroit who had you bound in a leather harness and suspended in air, removing his Rainbow flips and tying one to your face while you licked that sweatblackened foot imprint while he hung the other one from your dick by the toestrap. Do you like flip-flops now?"

"Fuck!" screamed Jon. "That was five years? Fuck, each one was hotter than the last. I fucking love flip-flops. I love sandals. Anything that shows off feet. Feet. I love feet." Jon seemed to be getting hornier and dumber by the second, jerking his member all the way through it, but still unable to nut.

"Calm down," Gage said, taking control of the situation, "take a look at my toes and find a sense of peace."

Jon looked and did so, almost instantly. His jerking became less forceful. He was in a good spot.

"Wow," he said, almost panting, "that thing you just did was ... intense."

"Imagine how it was for Mike," Gage said. "I could deal with him only so much, but at least left him with two things: the power of his feet to take over the minds of whomever was in his area and a quest to find someone much more suitable than he to take on the mantle."

"The mantle?" asked Jon, still gently jacking himself.

"Yes," said Gage. "Remember, Aizen can't travel to your realm. He wants to find someone to help achieve his goal of making everyone in the world cum and experience sexual fulfillment to its fullest. It'll literally save the human race -- and it's the best way to do it."

"This is a weird goal," Jon said, brazenly.

"Only weird 'cos no one who hears of this ever thinks it's gonna work," Gage said. "Think of Mike used that limited amount of power that he had for good. It's fine that he was a dick to you and your friends: he was testing all of you. Seeing if good can come out of so much sexual suffering. Your friends went through stuff against their will, but this may be the only time in your history where the ends justify the means. You were like if Job was cock-teased for 40 years. You could handle it. You have experienced the worst that these powers can offer, and that's why, Jon, you're going to use them for good."

Gage waved his hand, as if casting a spell. Suddenly, the constant jerking Jon was doing was leading to real feelings of pleasure. He was really, really enjoying it. He was ... working to get off.

"Jon," Gage said, "I am going to give you all the powers. You will be Aizen's ambassador to the world. You can change anyone's life for the sexual better, and you are going to give lust and satisfaction to so many people you won't even believe. You have seen the face of Footgod, and you are deemed worthy."

Jon was getting hornier the more he jacked it. "OK. This is ... yes, I accept."

"Good," Gage said, "now get on your knees."

Jon did so, his jacking dick perfectly positioned between Gage's jeans-covered knees.

"I think you'll be able to make it back here," started Gage, "but for now, I think you're going to find your new life something a whole lot better than anything you could've ever imagined. You thought you liked flip-flops? Wait until you experience everything that Aizen wants you to experience."

Gage pressed both his thumbs onto Jon's forehead and Jon's eyes practically went white, shooting out light as his mind and his dick were overwhelmed with hundreds of lifetimes worth of sexual experiences, each one more arousing than the last. Gage fed all of this into his brain, and Jon was cumming again and again and again in every scenario he ever lived out. He was bound spread eagle, he was spanked in public, he was raw-dogged, he was tickle tortured, he was -- sex. He was every sexy kinky thought anyone ever had, and now, as he was jacking in the void, he was getting closer and closer to cumming, right on the edge, oh fuck, there was no way to FUCK IT HE WAS GOING TO CUM NOW ...

CHAPTER VIII: FOOTGOD CUMMETH

"Whoa!" shouted Alex, Owen, and Atlan, almost in unison. Jon was shooting off rockets of cum so explosive they almost hit the ceiling of the apartment. Watching his cock pulse was truly a thing to behold, as it was flexing like a muscle as it prepared and fired out each rocket with an intensity that seemed, at least to the guys, superhuman. The first rocket legitimately hit the ceiling of the apartment -- they had never seen anything like it.

Everyone let Jon go. Mike turned off the buttplug. Everyone was in sheer awe of the overload of lust that was just displayed. It wasn't sex: it was beyond sex. It was something so much more ingrained inside the DNA of the universe than it was mere human function. There was something different about this. Something magical.

Jon stood up, and everyone stared: there was a hue around Jon. A slight, barely-noticeable aura of gold around the boy. His cock was still unrepentantly huge, but something about it shape, its form, its glow -- it was hypnotic. It was the one thing everyone wanted to stare at. God, it was just so beautiful.

Jon himself seemed in a state of discovery. He was elated due to the orgasm but also apparently feeling something he hadn't experienced before. He had a smile of disbelief, like realizing you have a winning lottery ticket in your hand and the doors of your mind opening in rapid succession with all the possibilities that lay before you. A stupid grin stretched across Jon's face, and it just grew into a smile: a big, goofy smile.

The guys stared. They had no idea what was happening but that cock was the most stunning thing they've ever seen with their eyes. The veins, the rim of the cockhead, the way the scrotum and balls compliment it so completely -- it was divine.

Jon started laughing to himself. The guys were taken off guard.

"Guys!" shared Jon, hard and happy, "I ... I have needed to have this foot fetish inside of me. I am so grateful it's inside of me. It's ... changed the way I see the fucking world. Goodness. It's a gospel, a mantra, a fucking life philosophy. Guys ... It's been in my head for fucking days but now I'm just learning to embrace it, and I am so, so, so very happy. This is the best I've ever felt ... ever! Ahhhh I want to scream!"

"Are ... are you OK, Jon?" asked Alex, curious and bursting through his cockcage.

"Oh, Alex," Jon said, standing, confident, glowing. "I can see it all, now. Aizen has shown me the way, and I am blessed with carrying out his dictum."

"Uhhhh, you're scaring me," said Michael, still unable to stop looking at Jon's gorgeous member.

Jon smirked. "Boys, I have seen it all. I have transcended, and I'm going to give all of you everything you've ever wanted. Here, let me show you. Alex, stand up straight."

Alex did so, his naked body covered by only his black cockcage and those raven locks on his head. Jon took one look at the chastity device and nodded his head -- and the guys turned their focus to Alex's crotch and were stunned to see the chastity cage simply evaporate into nothingness. Now free, Alex's thick dick, sensing cool air for the first time in a good while, got instantly hard. Alex instinctively touched himself and started jacking it. Jon walked over to him slowly, his bare feet making no sound on the ground as he went.

"Alex," Jon said, calmly. "Let's make it happen for you."

Jon pressed his thumb up on Alex's forehead, and both men seemingly went into a trance. For Alex, his mouth went agape, as if he had an onset orgasm come on, staggering back slightly. In that moment, Jon saw Alex's entire sexual history: his girlfriends, his good nights and bad nights, his attempts at fetishes and his preferences. Getting blown in public with the threat of getting caught was a fantasy for him. Going down on a girl was not his idea of a good time. He wondered what it'd be like if there was a collar around his neck and leash to pull him in a certain direction. There were some ideas and concepts he had in his head that were intriguing but not yet fully explored. Jon saw it all in a nanosecond.

And in the moment that followed, Jon took him through months of sexual fulfillment, but Jon put himself as the desirable creature in all those scenarios. He had Alex be his stay-at-home puppy, tail butt plug inserted in his behind, waiting for Master to get home and kissing the tops of his toes when he arrived. He made Alex get too drunk and forced to strip on a Facebook live video. They went walking in a garden one day and snuck behind the bushes, stripping themselves naked while Jon bent over and Alex ate him out, sticking his tongue farther down Jon's pink asshole than he ever thought possible. There was the footjob, the tit clamps, the late night cuddling -- all of it. Months of it. Over and over again.

In the next second in the real world, Alex's dick grew and hardened in fast-motion, turning red and seemingly driven by every horny force ever in the world. He collapsed to his knees -- Jon's thumb still on his forehead, 'cos he was expecting this -- and Alex quaked in ecstasy. It's like he had 1000 orgasms happen all at the same time. He shot a giant load right then and there, the look on his face that of someone who was just changed, radically.

Owen and Atlan stared in amazement. Jon himself seemed pretty amazed by what just happened as well. He had ... powers. He saw the needs and desires inside people and could unleash them. Unlock them. Enhance them. Every passing second was a new revelation for him. This was the lottery ticket: the infinite doors of erotic possibilities were presenting themselves.

With Alex collapsed in ecstasy on the floor, Jon glanced at Atlan and Owen. Without even touching them, Jon saw into their minds. There was Atlan, tied up and having his cock feather-edged for days at a time. Begging for permission to cum and never getting it. Being told to sit on a dildo "or else". It was all so master-slave, so vivid, so powerful. Then there was Owen: in a leather harness and leather pants, slaves tumbling over themselves to lick the soles of his bare feet. There he was tied up and being put in a milking machine, extracting cumshots out of him with merciless regularity. There was being hogtied with a hood over his head and being forgotten for long stretches of time. There was being blown as his dick was sticking through prison bars. There was breathplay. There were handcuffs. There were not-so-discreet confessions. It was all so spicy, so distinct.

Jon processed this information and waved his finger in the air. In an instant, both men felt an entire year's worth of cock edging without being able to get off and a separate entire year's worth of vibrating butt plug torture happen in their bodies at the same time. They both jerked at the hips, legs weak, feeling intense sensations all at the same time. Jon couldn't "see" the pleasure they were feeling inside their bodies, but could absolutely sense it. In one thought, he took these pleasurable sensations in their torsos -- which was also lighting up their brains -- and spread it around their entire bodies, both men now feeling sheer pleasure inside every molecule of their beings.

They both collapsed to the floor and twitched in erotic joy. Jon had never seen a thing like it: a full-blown body orgasm. It was insane and beautiful and erotic all at once. Jon just observed them as they were in the moment for a few minutes, before both of them "come down" from the experience. They were absolutely changed men.

And with that, Jon then turned to Mike, who, still in his business suit (save for his lack of shoes and socks), immediately got down on the floor in a bowing position towards Jon. He knew exactly what was going on.

"Sir," Mike started, "you saw what I had to do. This was all in an effort to find you." Mike started kissing the tops of Jon's bare, masculine feet, going from toe to toe with quick smooches and stopping only occasionally to speak.

"Forgiveness," Mike said, "forgiveness is all I ask. Please go easy on me. This was for the greater good. This was for Aizen."

Jon thought about Mike stopping his groveling and Mike suddenly did so. He thought Mike should be kneeling and look up to Jon which ... Mike then did. Jon's powers apparently extended to the subconscious.

"Don't bring up Aizen's name," Jon said. "He gave you a gift that you abused."

"But I found you," Mike pleaded, eyes looking desperate. "It was all in an effort to find someone who could meet him."

Jon smirked. "Find me you did ... but at the cost of so many other people's lives. Come with me."

At that moment, Jon pressed his thumb onto the forehead of the kneeling Mike and saw his entire sexual past and history, which, given what powers he had been blessed with, was far more intense than those fantasies of Atlan or Owen or Alex. Jon saw Patrick and Brian and Dan and Nathan. Jon closed his eyes which lead to Mike closing his eyes. Jon took one breath, opened his eyes, and saw that he and Mike were in the middle of Mike's home-base.

"Whoa!" Dan said, in front of the computer, doing a web show. He stood up, hard, now out of frame of the camera. Brian, Nathan, and Patrick were all subconsciously rubbing their cock cages as they were watching Dan get off but now were looking at Master Mike suddenly in the room and ... kneeling. And ... wasn't that the guy they were looking up the social media profiles for? Jon? Why was Jon naked and ... was he glowing? Just a bit. Their eyes all fixated on Jon's gorgeous cock.

"So," Jon said, "these are the boys."

"Yes, Sir," said Mike. His mere use of the word "Sir" intrigued all of the men that Mike had under his control. Was their Master ... no longer the Master?

Jon quickly read the minds of everyone in the room. He saw what Mike had put them through. Jon nodded, realizing that his actions would, in fact, be justified.

"Fellas," Jon said, growing more comfortable in his role, "today's your day."

With a mere thought, the cock cages on Patrick, Brian, and Nathan melted away, dripping into nothingness. The boys grew rather hard rather quickly, pleasing Jon. They all started stroking themselves while staring at Jon's godlike erection.

"Mike was using you," Jon declared, "in order to try and get to me. He has made you all do things you would rather not and forcing you into foreign pleasures that are not your own. I am here to fix that."

Mike suddenly had a panicked look in his eyes. "Goodness no, please!" Mike screamed.

"Mike," Jon started, recognizing that every word he was about to speak was to be received as gospel. "You are now enslaved to Patrick, Brian, Nathan, and Dan. They will control you for as long as I see fit. They are free to go about their own volition. They will leave this apartment tonight, never to return -- but they can call on you at any time for anything with no hesitation."

All the boys were getting very excited at such a thought. Their stroking increased. Genuine smiles grew on their faces -- a limitless line of possibilities laid out before them. This was their moment.

"Go ahead," Jon said, "try it out."

Dan, in his simple monotone voice, wasted no time. "Crawl over here, boy," Dan commanded. Mike tried to look at Jon for mercy but the commands of Dan took over, and without hesitation he started slowly crawling on all fours over to the recently-freed horndog slaves. They soon formed a circle around him.

"Now strip!" Patrick commanded, and Mike started slowly removing his clothes, eyes big and puppy-dog like. This subconscious plea was met with no audience. The guys were in charge now.

Jon intervened. "Patrick, come here," he said. Patrick walked over. Jon thought for a second and suddenly Patrick was dressed in cargo shorts, a T-shirt of a band he liked, and thin white ankle socks. Patrick always felt sexy when he was casual, so Jon made that simple wish come true.

"Guys," Jon said to Dan, Brian, and Nathan. "You got 10 years with him. Have fun."

Apparently, nothing else needed to be said, because the guys knew what to do: Mike was kneeling in front of his former captives and they all pressed their thumbs to his forehead and proceeded to mentally put Mike through an entire decade of erotic torments. There was humiliation: there was him entering a nude wrestling ring with muscles writhing and sweating and him losing the match and being forced to suck the dick of the winner in the ring. There was being frozen as a statue with a pair of hands lovingly fondling his nipples for months on end, his horniness increasing but not able to get off. There was Dan tying up Mike and leaving him propped up against a couch while sitting on the floor, Dan shoving his ass in Mike's face and Mike being forced to lick Dan's asshole until he learned to love it. And forced costumes. And facing a genuine fucking machine. And two unstoppable years of cum-free tickle torture, his body left writhing at the end of it with shockwaves of laughter coming out of him for weeks after it ended.

And that was just the start. The boys, in the course of seconds, were torturing their former tormentor for everything he did to them, and they were going to enjoy themselves. Jon and Patrick looked at their smiles and could see that this was part of their healing process, and they were going to make full use of it.

Jon started walking out of the process and a sock-footed Patrick followed, going down the wooden staircase of the third-floor walk-up and chatting politely. Jon was outdoors and still completely naked, that glow around him actually highlighting his every surrounding.

"Patrick, you've had it rough," Jon started. "Your escape attempt broke my heart. You are free now."

"And I want a boyfriend," Patrick volunteered, the words surprising him as they slipped out his mouth.

"I know," said Jon, "and I want you with me. I've seen every single sexual experience there is in this universe and I want to experience them all over again, but with passion behind it. I want to go around this globe and get people in a better place, let their sexual freedom shape their worldviews into something positive. I want you to be there for that."

Patrick was in genuine awe, barely processing everything that was happening, but went with his gut instinct: "You got it, Sir."

"Please ... call me Jon."

"Sure thing ... Jon," Patrick started, a bit of a giddy thrill in his face. They held hands as they were walking down the street.

"So, uh," Patrick asked, sheepishly, still happy that his long-dormant secret of wanting a boyfriend now being realized in front of him, "who do we pick first to change their lives?"

"Well," Jon started, "I can't see everyone in the world's sexual energies all at once, but I can see people around me. This house over here?" Jon said while pointing, "is occupied by a frat boy who's made some bad decisions but has some kinks that could be turned into something really compelling."

"So ... we just walk in?" Patrick asked.

"No," Jon smiled, "we should be polite. Let's make this happen."

Without a second thought, a nude Jon and a sock-footed Patrick walked up to this house that Jon knew would have a man inside who was about to go through the sexual journey of his lifetime.

Jon rapped his had against the door. On the other side, the drunken fratboy and his roommates just heard three. sharp. knocks.

BONUS STORY: ETERNAL BONDAGE

The wedding rings clicked together.

Here Eli was, tuxedo mostly removed, being taken from behind by Jim. They were deep in the throes of drunken passion, feeling lust to the nth degree, their bodies surging with pleasure. After all: they were just married hours ago.

Now, after fumbling most of their finely tailored suits off, these two young guys were enjoying the kind of passion that only comes from a deep emotional connection. There was Eli, bent over the bed in their newlywed suite, issuing moans as his big booty was receiving his husband's diamond-hard cock. Jim was drunk and horned up, leaning over Eli to give him no space to move. His hands were pressed on top of Eli's hands, the force of each thrust making their wedding bands click together. They were sweaty, stupid, and passionate. It was great.

"You like that, boy?" Jim got out between thrusts, stabbing his beet-red veiny cock deep into Eli's eager hole.

"YES DADDY" squeaked out Eli, his pounded prostate feeling on fire with desire.

The boys were so hot for each other, happy to finally escape the months of wedding planning, the best man toasts, and the dancefloor congratulations from drunken college friends. They were now giving into their animalistic lust for each other and loving every fucking minute of it.

"I think I'm gonna cum, daddy!" screamed Eli.

"Fuck, *I'm* gonna cum" yelled Jim.

And almost at the same time, the newlyweds shot their pent-up leads, with Jim pumping pulse after pulse of semen directly into Eli's tight ass, just as Eli shot rockets of his hot cum directly into the side of this fancy hotel room mattress.

Jim was still inserted when all was said and done, the couple heaving in a post-coital glow. They were happy but goddamn exhausted, the passion and the stress of the big day having worn on them pretty heavily.

Jim pulled out, stood up, and flopped backwards onto their large wedding bed, landing on his back and almost instantly closing his eyes. As Eli, after composing himself, got up and went to the bathroom to get tissues to clean up all this sticky manseed, Jim could feel himself already drifting off into exhaustion-powered sleep.

"I love you," he muttered out to Eli, the powers of unconsciousness soon taking over. The last sensation he remembered was the feeling of Eli, being the sweetheart that he is, wiping down his dick. Just ... the best possible husband in the universe.

Jim slept for at least 10 hours that night.

+ + +

Jim awoke in a daze. There were little slits of sunlight peeking in through the closed windows of the newlyweds' hotel room, but they provided only minimal illumination. Jim tasted something in his mouth ... but he couldn't place it. Something tangy and salty and sweet. Something ... made of cotton?

Jim's eyes went wide. It was a sock. But ... he couldn't spit it out. It was lodged in there. He tried to reach over and take the sock out ... but he couldn't move his arm. Hell, he couldn't move his leg. He tried to frantically assess his surroundings, and it soon dawned on him: he was completely fucked.

He was laying spread eagle on a bed, tied very tightly to the bedposts on the floor. He could barely move a muscle. In his mouth was a plastic gag that had a bit of a knob going into the mouth, making it difficult to form sounds of any sort. Attached to that was a smelly sock that was getting wetter by the second with Jim's saliva.

Worst of all, however, was his midsection. In his ass he felt a butt plug, but the kind that went in only a part of the way: it was the kind of rubbery thing that was designed to specifically not reach the prostate. This wasn't designed for pleasure: this was designed for frustration and torment.

On Jim's crotch, however, was the worst thing of all: a shiny metal cock cage. He must've passed out hard, because it is truly amazing he didn't wake up to the sensations of his cock being diligently shoved inside. It was a nightmare.

"Good morning, honey!" shouted Eli, walking into the room completely naked, already half hard. "How are you?"

Jim strained at his restraints, trying to scream "WHAT THE FUCK!" There was a panic in his eyes. Eli seemed to blissfully ignore it.

"Oh, looks like you got yourself a little tied up last night, didn't you?" smirked Eli. Jim mumbled something in reply.

Without hesitation, Eli jumped on the bed and straddled his newly minted husband, his butt bouncing on top of Jim's cockcage. Eli then dug right into Jim's ribs with his fingers. Jim's eyes went wide with ticklish sensation and the muffled screaming started.

Every muscle of Jim's pulled at his restraints with all their might but the laughs just kept coming: Eli's fingernails were at the perfect length where his tips could dive in without poking but he could also scratch like a motherfucker. The tickling was so surprising and intense that Jim's brain could barely catch up.

"Don't worry, baby," Eli started, "this is just to wear you out. With all of this pulling on your restraints, I'd hate to have you keep fighting me as I lay things out for you."

Jim closed his eyes as hard as he could, as if trying to wish the torment away, but Eli's fingers were too good, too devious to let him rest for a second. Every time a tickle spot had been worn out, it instinctually found another one. It was almost inhuman, and Jim's body exercised every single ounce of energy it had at its disposal to try and resist the attack -- all for naught.

This continued for a good 20 minutes.

By the time Eli stopped, Jim was heaving through his sockgag. He was exhausted already, droplets of sweat appearing on his body. Eli dismounted off of his husband and laid to this side, looking at him sweetly as those devious hands worked their way up to Jim's nipples and started lightly fondling them.

"Oh, does this get you horny, Jim?" asked Eli with a wicked grin. "Is your cock cage starting to fill up?" Jim let out a moan of frustration, but Eli kept going.

"Jim, I don't know what you think you're doing here, but I'm going to break you. I'm going to get you so filled with pleasure you're going to break. You see, now that we're finally together, bound by law, I aim to get the most out of my man. I'm not gonna have some sort of marriage where we fuck for the first year and then things go dry after that, no. I'm gonna own you, tease, you, torment you, and make you heel. You'll soon be at my heels."

All Jim could do is moan. Eli stood up on the bed and lightly pressed on the cockcage with his foot.

"Oh, is there something in here that wants to come out?" Eli teased. Jim mumbled something in a very defeated tone.

"Just so you know, I had this made custom," Eli explained. "It says 'Eli's Backup Cock' on it -- 'cos that's what it is. You're not gonna get to cum for days on end, honey. Only when I decide you can."

Another muffled, anguished scream from Jim. Eli moved a bit and soon pressed his big wide size 11 bare foot onto Jim's face.

"Sniff it," Eli said, sternly. Jim tried to struggle but soon the toes were forceful enough to hold his face in place, keeping it there long enough that Jim had no choice but to take a breath -- and again, that foot scent entered his brain right away.

"Your foot fetish is so cute to me," Eli said, still holding Jim's face in place with his toes. "I'm thinking that every day I get home from work, you'll untie my shoes for me and then peel off my socks at my command. I'll make the determinations though: I know how much you love my feet, how hard your foot fetish gets you, so every day when we're back from our jobs, no matter how stressful, you're going to obey me. Maybe I'll make you sniff 'em. Maybe I won't. All I know is that it'll be a weekday, so you won't be out of your cock cage one bit. Maybe when my socks are off, I'll make you kneel and take some nipple teases. Or some tickles. Probably nipple teases. I want my husbandboy obedient. Doesn't that sound great?"

Jim let out another sad muffled sigh.

"Ooh, and maybe we can have friends over!" said Eli with a menacing delight in his voice. "Hot guys whom I can snuggle up with on the couch and make out with as both pairs of feet are out on the coffee table, and you'll be ordered to service them both, licking over and over and me and my friends get off and you remain hard in a cage. Doesn't that sound just grand?"

Jim almost-screamed through his gag. He was so weak now, it barely even mattered. He was succumbing to his husband's devious plan against his will.

"That's right, boy," said Eli, now getting back to laying on the bed and playing with those nipples. "I'm gonna make you squirm. I'm gonna fuck you and get off when I want to … and you're just gonna take it. This is gonna be a great marriage and we'll have a lot of fun -- but first I'm gonna need to break you in."

Eli got up and started putting clothes on. Jim looked over at him, tied, muzzled, caged, and concerned. Eli didn't care, getting in casual wear and putting on slippers. He grabbed his room card key from the end table.

"I'm hungry from tickling you so much! I'm going to go get a continental breakfast. I'll bring you back something. Hope I don't take too long, 'cos you'll be suffering through this …"

With that, Eli took out a very small remote control that he had and pressed a button. This caused Jim's buttplug to start vibrating, keeping his tight little asshole awake and alert at all moments. Given it was short enough to not touch the prostate, this created a feeling of frustration the likes of which he couldn't believe. His body wanted to explode with pleasure right now but there was no way for him to get that release. He screamed and writhed and stared at his husband with puppy dog eyes.

"Maybe I'll leave the remote here?" Eli dropped it on the floor. "See you in an hour ..."

BONUS STORY: LET ME IN

There it was, the house. The one from the photo.

Slave was looking out the window of the bus and felt his heart pounding as it drew to a stop on the road. It was a non-descript property, but it also was facing the beach and the ocean. This was a house of money. This was a house of power.

Slave was in a foreign state, full of cum, and worried as he was excited. It was such a risk. No one knew he was here. He had never met a Master who lived in another state, but there was a connection with this one, and the many chats and photo exchanges and tasks and fantasy-shares had driven slave to whole new levels of curiosity. Yet here he was now, getting out of a bus in the midday California sun, about to walk to a new location and suffer a host of new consequences.

He looked both ways and moved across the crosswalk. The sound of the waves crashing against the beach and people talking and frolicking gave a sense of comfort, but Slave's mind kept wandering. For some reason, he could see himself on that beach later ... naked ... on all fours ... lead by a leash and collar.

Slave approached the door of Master's house. He rang the buzzer and looked back at the sidewalk behind him. He didn't even know what he was looking for. An escape route? People in case things went awry? It was weird being in a non-private location for a sexual encounter. Why wasn't the door opening? He pressed the buzzer again. He didn't want to seem impatient, but--

"Hello, Slave," said a voice over an intercom.

"Hello, Sir. Please let me in," the Slave started, stammering a bit, nervous.

"No," said the intercom voice. "You must prove to me that you want in and to go under my control."

"Sir," Slave pleaded, "I'm here in a foreign state and I'm here, isn't that enough?"

"No," the voice said. "Do you want to go under my control or not, boy? I'm more than happy to never open this door for you and you go on your merry way, all frustrated and untamed."

Slave groaned to himself. He knew this was a good Master. This was an exacting Master.

"What do you want, Sir?" Slave asked.

"There's a video camera above the door, and I'm watching and recording you. Don't think you can get anything past me, OK?"

"OK," said the Slave.

"Now ... take off your shirt, Slave."

Slave felt OK with this command and removed it right away. He was in California after all. Lots of shirtless dudes everywhere. He dropped it on the porch.

"Now, take off your pants, boy."

Slave was a bit more hesitant about this one, but, again, it was California. He had boxers on. This perhaps wasn't the most unusual sight in the world for a resident. He took his socks off too for good measure. He took his pants and folded them in his arms.

"No no," the intercom voice said. "You thought you were going to take those in here? When you come in here, you will have nothing from the outside world to please you. I'll collect those later ... if I deem fit."

"But, my wallet and phone are in--"

"I mean, you can go home if you want, boy," the intercom voice interrupted. Slave sighed. He knew this was the only way.

"Yes, Sir," he moaned.

"Good boy," the voice said. "Now, drop those shorts."

Slave hesitated. Sure, the porch was a bit off of the road and sidewalk, but ... he had never felt so exposed or vulnerable. He realized this was going to be the biggest dive into sexual pleasure he had ever taken, but his new Master was going to be more than happy to push his limits ... and his buttons.

With great reluctance, Slave slid them off and faced the door of Master's home, naked, ass cheeks facing the sidewalk, road, beach, and the world. He had never been naked in public possibly ever. It was terrifying and a bit thrilling too.

"Please, let me in, Sir," Slave pleaded. All he could hear from the intercom was cackling. The Master was really getting off on this.

"You're so close," the voice said. "You just need to do one last thing before I permit you entry into my world."

"What's that?" inquired the Slave, eyes darting to the sides to see if there was anyone behind him.

"I want you to get hard for me," commanded the voice.

There was a pause. Slave was taking a moment to digest this all. He felt a lot of things but was 100% not in the mood to be sexy right now. His limits had already been pushed enough. He was already naked in public. The last thing he needed to be was ... naked *and hard* in public.

"Sir, I think we've reached a limit," Slave said, getting desperate. "I'm here and I'm naked. Please let me in. Please, I don't want someone to see me."

"Slave," the voice said, "every pedestrian who walks by and sees your cute ass is someone you've never met before nor will ever see again. If you want to submit, you must do so wholly and completely. Once you're diamond-fucking-hard, I will let you in."

Slave was grabbing and tugging his dick, but it was like taffy, stretching and being profoundly unhard right now.

"Uhh, I don't think it's gonna happen, Sir," Slave admitted, getting more desperate to not be exposed to the world by the second.

"It's OK, Slave," said the voice. "I expected this to happen. That's why I prepared a little gift for you. Open up the mailbox next to the door."

Slave opened up the black wall-mounted metal mailbox and felt something inside. He pulled it out. It was a zip-lock bag containing ... Master's worn ankle socks.

"Don't worry, boy," the voice said. "They're not too rank. Just rank enough, as you've described for me. Worn for three days. I know you're nervous, but I know you've been wanting to smell these for weeks on end. So do me a favor: close your eyes, forget where you are, and open it up and take a whiff."

Slave was worried he had already been standing on the porch naked for too long and was absolutely sure at least someone had seen him in a state of undress. However, the only way out is through, and Slave sucked up his pride to make this happen. He took a big gulp of breath, opened up the bag, and lifted it to his nose.

Sniff.

In that one moment, masculine pheromones entered his skull. There was a flavor, a taste to it all. This wasn't just socks: it was the captured scene of a male essence. Dominant, powerful, controlling. In that one whiff, Slave felt that ting of electricity in his groin -- the kind that leads to an erection. It felt so good.

"Do you like?" asked the intercom.

"Yes, very much so," sighed Slave.

"You like being under control of masculine, male bare feet, don't you?"

Slave took another whiff and was stiffening. "Yes, Sir. I really do love it."

"You're a little slut, aren't you Footpig?" asked the voice. "A glutton for sexy punishment."

The voice was saying all the right things. Slave was jacking now.

"Take another whiff, you whore," the voice commanded. Slave took another inhale and felt his whole body come to a submissive state of peace. Here he was, naked, in public, jerking himself to his Master's used socks and genuinely enjoying it.

"Stop for a second and let me see that dick on camera," the voice ordered. Slave stopped and wasn't sure exactly where the camera was located but apparently, it was good enough. "Yes, you're rock hard, aren't you boy?"

"Yes, Sir," Slave moaned.

"Do you want to get harder?"

"Yes, Sir," Slave nodded.

"Keep sniffing. Keep jacking. Keep thinking about how much you want to serve my sexy male bare feet and toes and soles ..."

"Yes, Sir," Slave said, his stroking and tugging getting furiouser and furiouser, each new intake of breath getting another whiff of those sexy smelly socks.

"You're such a fucking footperv, aren't you?" the voice asked.

"YES!" Slave said as he took another breath, getting harder. Who the fuck cared if anyone saw him now? He was living his best--

"Enter," the voice said. A buzzing sound happened at the door, meaning it was unlocked. Slave entered as quickly as he could, closing the door behind him. He was in a small (and very clean) mudroom, with another door. He entered through that one, socks in one hand, rock hard dick in the other. Facing him was his Master, the one he had been chatting online forever. He was in a reclining comfort chair, leaning back and legs propped up. Sticking out of those jeans and facing the Slave were the sexiest pair of male soles and toes he had ever seen. Slave didn't even realize that he was still jerking himself as he stared, naked, with socks in one hand.

"Now," the Master said, "we can begin."

STILL FOOTHORNY?

Don't forget to try out these other James T. Medak classics!

- **GETTING OFF ON THE WRONG FOOT (2013)**

  The start of a new era: a collection of fun, freaky, foot-centric fetish stories designed to rock your socks off -- but why were you wearing socks in the first place, pray tell?

- **HOW TO BE A FOOTPIG (2014)**

  At long last, a full-length gay foot fetish novel featuring a college student with one too many horny secrets on his laptop and the fraboys who discover it. One of the foothorniest novels ever.

- **THE BEST FOOT FORWARD: The James T. Medak Anthology (2014)**

  Unsure of where to start in diving into the tomes of James T. Medak? Try this overview from all of Medak's writings over the years, from the early Forum stories of extensive tickle torture to brand-new exclusives dealing with edging, bondage, and outright foot domination. They're all here, ready for your eager eyes (and raging footboner).

Enjoy!

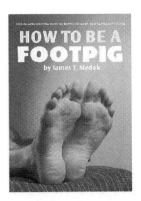
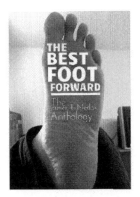

All books available from JTM Services, Inc. and can be found where ever fine horny books (or ebooks) are sold. Enjoy, pigs.

Made in the USA
Columbia, SC
27 February 2019